W9-BJD-715

Smoke

and Other Early Stories

Smoke

and Other Early Stories

by *Djuna Barnes*

edited, with an Introduction

by Douglas Messerli

College Park, Maryland

SUN & MOON PRESS

1982

© Sun & Moon Press, 1982

These stories previously appeared in *All Story Cavalier Weekly*, *The Trend*, and the *New York Morning Telegraph Sunday Magazine*.

The cover drawing and other illustrations are by Djuna Barnes.

Publication of this book has been made possible, in part, by a grant from the National Endowment for the Arts.

Library of Congress Cataloging in Publication Data

Barnes, Djuna. 1892-1982
  Smoke and other early stories.

  Includes bibliographical references.
  I. Messerli, Douglas, 1947-
II. Title.
PS3503.A614S6 1982 813'.52 82-10627
ISBN 0-940650-17-7
ISBN 0-940650-12-6 (pbk.)

10 9 8 7 6 5 4 3
First Edition

Sun & Moon Press
4330 Hartwick Road
College Park, Maryland 20740

Acknowledgments

The work and talents of several individuals helped to bring together this collection. As Associate Editor, Alyce Barry worked on all aspects of publication, from helping to select the stories and copyediting to typesetting and proofreading. With her usual perfection and extraordinary patience, Barbara Shaw did the layout of the book, aided by Paul Moran. Kevin Osborn advised on design of the book and coordinated its printing. And Howard N. Fox had the unenviable task of editing the editor. I extend my warmest thanks to these people.

My thanks also go to the librarians and staffs of The Library of Congress and the University of Maryland Library Special Collections, who helped me in obtaining most of these materials.

Douglas Messerli

in memory of Djuna Barnes

The Newspaper Tales of Djuna Barnes

Writing in the introduction to *Djuna Barnes: A Bibliography,* I noted in 1975 that, while several essays had been devoted to Barnes' masterpiece, *Nightwood,* the full range of her writing had yet to be discussed. Barnes' other longer works, *Ryder* and *The Antiphon,* had received only cursory treatment, while her short fictions, dramas, poems, and journalism had been virtually ignored. In the seven years since that assessment, critical books by Louis Kannenstine[1] and James B. Scott[2] have been published on most aspects of Barnes' writing, and a biography by Andrew Field is promised for the near future. These books, along with several new essays and dissertations focusing on various of her works and the reprinting of her *Ladies Almanack* (Harper & Row, 1972), *Ryder* (St. Martin's, 1979) and *Selected Works* (Farrar, Straus & Giroux, 1980) represent what clearly is the beginnings of a reevaluation of one of the major literary innovators of the twentieth century.

It remains, however, that little has been written on Barnes' short fictions, poems, and dramas. But considering the fact

---

[1]Louis F. Kannenstine, *The Art of Djuna Barnes: Duality and Damnation* (New York: New York University Press, 1977).

[2]James B. Scott, *Djuna Barnes* (Boston: G. K. Hall Co./Twayne, 1976).

that, until this publication, only one slim volume of her shorter works has been kept in print, such inattention is not surprising. The twelve stories, assorted poems, and dramas first collected in *A Book* in 1923 and reprinted with three additional tales in *A Night Among the Horses* in 1929, were winnowed down to ten revised stories in *Spillway* in 1962, only nine of which found their way into *Selected Works* in the same year. In other words, so few of Barnes' shorter writings have been available, that only a handful of readers have been aware of her total contribution. *Smoke and Other Early Stories* is the first in a series of new volumes to be published by Sun & Moon Press of Barnes' fiction, drama, poetry, and journalism in an attempt to provide a clearer picture of her literary career.

These various writings were begun in 1913, when, at the age of 21, Barnes hired on as a feature writer for the Brooklyn *Daily Eagle*. In the next six years—in the *Eagle*, the New York *Press, Telegraph, World* and other City newspapers—she published more than one hundred feature articles and interviews on celebrities of the day, among them such disparate personages as Lillian Russell, Florenz Ziegfeld, David Belasco, "Mother" Jones, Billy Sunday, and Alfred Stieglitz. This prodigious output is made to seem even more extraordinary by the fact that, beginning in 1916, Barnes contributed to the *New York Morning Telegraph Sunday Magazine* a series of twenty-five dramas and fictions. Eleven of these fictions plus three others that had appeared earlier in *All Story Cavalier Weekly* and *The Trend* make up this volume.

Readers today may find it difficult to imagine how the mass audience of a newspaper that in its later years marketed itself as New York's "racing sheet," would or even *could* have responded to fictions so peculiar as these, with their radical metaphors ("...Paprika had a moribund mother under the counterpane, a chaperone who never spoke or moved, since she was paralyzed, but who was a pretty good one at that, being a white exclamation point this side of error."); their oracular observations ("When a woman decides to lie down and play 'possum, she always selects with fearful care her hosiery, her petticoats and her shoes."); and their artificial dialogue ("He walks like a cat. I do not like it. ...A little dusty cat, with a gray nose from prowling in among what people call great facts. Why, will you tell me, have all great things to be dusted? Cathedrals and books and windmills?"). Several of these tales are so startlingly eccentric that, even in a century characterized by its literary experimentation, it is difficult to place them in the Modernist context.

The fact that these tales first appeared in a newspaper, accordingly, today may seem as odd as if one were to encounter the work of Thomas Pynchon or Kathy Acker in the pages of the New York *Post.* But in 1916, the American newspaper was a remarkably eclectic forum, and fiction and drama were standard features. Although today we retain some of the remnants of that eclecticism in our style and entertainment sections that feature everything from political memoirs to medical advice, the newspapers of Barnes' day often imported the very language of popular entertainment into the news items of the front pages. Hence, Barnes' audience may have been more prepared for the sensationalized metaphors, authorial intrusions, and theatrical dialogue of her stories than we are, en-

countering them now in our narrower and often more aca-
demic literary context. And it is clear that just as her audience may have been primed by the journalistic context in
which these tales were presented, Barnes herself adopted certain narrative conventions from the reportorial journalism of
her day. Of particular importance are the several ways in
which the presentational devices of journalism are manifested
in these fictions through Barnes' approaches to character,
voice, and plot.

Throughout her writing career, Barnes has employed her
figures as emblems, caricatures, and stereotypes that have
their roots in the character typologies of the literature of the
seventeenth and eighteenth centuries. But in these early
newspaper works this method of characterization may have
been less a conscious decision of Barnes to draw on previous
literary traditions than it was a convention of her medium.
Despite the increasing popularity of psychologically "round-
ed" characterizations in fiction as established by Henry James,
Knut Hamsun, Marcel Proust, and others, the American
newspaper feature-writing of the second decade of this century had not relinquished entirely the character types used by
writers such as Theodore Dreiser and Emile Zola. For instance,
Barnes wrote of such types in several of her articles in the
Daily Eagle[1] and for the same paper she made a series of

---

[1]In several of her feature articles, Barnes created a fictional figure,
Reginald Delancey, a dandyish, man-about-town. See "You Can
Tango—a Little—at Arcadia Dance Hall...," Brooklyn *Daily Eagle,*

twenty-four drawings titled "Types Found in Odd Corners Round About Brooklyn," which included sketches of stock figures such as the "Newsboy," the "Society Matron," and the "Vagrant." The characters of Barnes' newspaper tales, in turn, are grounded in Naturalism to the extent that they reflect ideas of environment and heredity that had been assimilated into journalistic thought. In "Smoke" the mother fears that instead of her husband having inherited "iron" in his veins, "there's a little blood." In "A Sprinkle of Comedy" a father unsuccessfully attempts to prevent his son from repeating his own past. In "The Coward," the very fact that Varra Kolveed has had a reputation all her life for courage, leads her to accomplish a courageous act. Throughout, these fictions are imbued with a sense of inevitability, are inhabited by figures that seemingly are determined by their genetic and environmental inheritances. Less than a total commitment to Naturalism, Barnes' characterizations nonetheless reveal her appropriation of the popular psychological and sociological notions of her day. When one reads of her "terrorists," "cowards," and "revolutionists," in short, one must understand them as par-

---

June 29, 1913, Part Four, p. 22 and "Twingless Twitchell and His Tantalizing Tweezers," Brooklyn *Daily Eagle*, July 27, 1913, Part Two, p. 6. In other articles such as "Who's the Last Squatter? Feud Rifts Pigtown Lute...," Brooklyn *Daily Eagle*, November 2, 1913, Part Two, p. 2, Barnes uses the very figures on whom she is reporting as stock dramatic types, portraying them with epithets such as "The Buxom Woman" and "The Lady Across the Cut."

ticipating in the milieu of popular newspaper sterotypes, as sharing in the landscape of the headline "killer," "judge," and "cop."

For similar reasons, Barnes felt no obligation in her stories to maintain the objective point of view—that realist convention of authorial exclusion which by mid-century had metamorphosed into dogma. As a feature writer Barnes could make no pretense that she was not the source of what she reported; and, as a fiction writer Barnes apparently saw no reason to abandon such a rhetorical approach, particulary since her informational asides often contributed to the sense of the inevitability of events. In "The Jest of Jests," in fact, Barnes begins with the traditional journalese naming of "who," "where," "what," and "when," which pervades the story with a sense of authorial control:

> The name of the heroine of this story is the Madelonette. Why never seemed to matter any more than that the hero should have been called the Physician when he had never so much as seen a case of measles in his life.
>
> The place of climax is Long Beach, but you will not undertand until you reach the very end, though I might as well warn you that it was there the Madelonette and the Physician fell into each other's arms, much to the consternation of the "regulars" on the boardwalk.

Although this fiction is the most determinist-oriented of her short works, nearly all the stories of this collection, through informational asides, directions to the reader, and other narrational manipulations, *expose the author as the source of the story*, as the apparent agent of a series of shared events. Even Barnes' use of the oracular voice, which might appear out of place in reportage, shares something in common with the editorial page; just as editorials often proclaim a knowledge of the general good in order to support a specific cause, so Barnes' tales lay claim to a knowledge of basic human behavior in order to support her specific narrative descriptions. In "A Sprinkle of Comedy," for example, Barnes observes:

> This man's [Roger's] friends were of the type that in an instant descend from "friend" into a "gang."
> It takes circumstance alone to make them either friend, lover, enemy, thief, brawler, what-not. It may be a hand on the shoulder, a word whispered in the ear, a certain combination of apparently unimportant incidents.

Through such commentaries and interruptions, Barnes makes it clear that she is the sole reporter/author of the tale she tells. Almost as if to demonstrate that the media often causes the events it reports, Barnes continually reminds her reader that without her "report," without her creation of these figures, there would be no story.

These tales, moreover, are structured in a manner similar to a news report. Beginning with an introductory paragraph or two in which location, characters, and action are established, the stories generally proceed in chronological order. Seldom do they demonstrate any of the literary techniques—radical shifts in time and place, stops in narrative action, and displacement of character—which distinguish what Joseph Frank has described as the "spatial structure" of Barnes' later work.[1] Rather, in these early fictions there is a clear connection between cause and effect. Coherent with its thematics of determinism, the structure of most of these tales is almost ploddingly grounded in the logical order of events.

For all this, few of these stories end in real dramatic closure. Although the destinies of the characters are determined, most of these tales are not resolved. In "Who Is This Tom Scarlett?" for example, the reader certainly suspects that Tom will be assimilated into the "gravy-spilling bourgeoise," but the story ends abruptly and it is uncertain whether the character will even survive. Although Varra Kolveed of "The Coward" proves her courage, the reader has no clear idea of what that means in terms of her life; is she arrested?; how does her confession affect Monk, the man who she detests? The reader of "What Do You See, Madam?" is frustrated completely in his desire to learn what happens to the central character, Mamie Saloam. The lives of these figures, just as the lives of those described on the front pages of the newspaper, may be determined, but are left incomplete. As in the news report, the

---

[1] Joseph Frank, *The Widening Gyre: Crisis and Mastery in Modern Literature* (New Brunswick, New Jersey: Rutgers University Press, 1963), pp. 43-66.

event—the murder, the capture, the trial, whatever—does not represent a denouement as much as it does a necessary place to stop. Accordingly, in Barnes' tales, as in the reports of the front-page criminals and disaster victims, incident prevails over both character and theme. History is unimportant except for how it relates to the action; although the characters' destinies are sealed, the reader is seldom permitted to experience the results.

To comprehend the significance of this emphasis on action in process, one need only compare these short works with those of Joyce's *The Dubliners* of two years earlier—the prototype, it is often argued, of the Modern short story. In fictions such as "Araby" and "A Little Cloud" action is relatively unimportant; in each of these stories, in fact, the plot is almost nonexistent. In "Araby" a young boy waits for and eventually is granted permission to attend a church bazaar, which, by the time he reaches it, is nearly closed. The action of the other story consists of Little Chandler conversing over drinks with his friend, Ignatius Gallaher, and later, screaming at his child, who reacts in tears. Certainly these synopses are oversimplified, but most readers would agree, I think, that the importance of these tales does not lie in the plot. Rather, the focus of Joyce's short fictions is the characters and their psychology. The incidents merely serve as symbols of their conditions. The closing of the bazaar, the crying of the child, are less significant as events than they are as images of the worlds which the characters inhabit. In Joyce's stories, in short, plot is no longer animus, but is revelation.

In Barnes' more journalistic approach, on the other hand,

nearly everything revolves around plot. If the characters seem sketchy, it is because they, rather than their actions, are the images of the condition of their kind. And it is only through their actions that significant meaning can occur. Indeed, Barnes sets up circumstances for her characters to insure that they act. In "A Night in the Woods," for example, Barnes stages the scene for the imprisonment of her figures in the most incidental of manners:

> And then the crash comes. A man and his wife somewhere on the border of the town die suddenly, and the cause has been traced back to poison found in a loaf of bread. As Jennie and Trenchard are the only bakers in the town they are immediately pounced upon by the marshall, and both of them landed securely in...jail.

What matters most for Barnes is not that they are imprisioned or even whether they will succeed in their attempt to escape, but *that they must attempt to escape*. The author has placed them in prison so that they can act, so that they will run. Once again, the reader cannot be certain of the result. In this fiction as in most of the tales of *Smoke and Other Early Stories*, it is action which reveals the living beings of which her figures are merely emblems. Tragedy, for Barnes, is inaction as demonstrated in the title story, in which the younger generation forgets how to act.

In short, the very qualities which help to make these tales seem so eccentric—the use of flat, stereotyped characters, the narrational intrusions, and the emphasis on unresolved narrative action—may have as much to do with where or when Barnes published them as with any decision to write peculiar or obscure fictions. At the same time, it is also clear that Barnes was not completely naive in her use of journalistic techniques. Her adaption of reportorial procedures to fiction was not an end in itself. For underlying her focus on action and her use of character typologies, the oracular voice, and narrative intrusions is Barnes' deeper commitment to an exploration of the moral condition of humankind. And in this concern she far transcends her newspaper model.

In Barnes' later works she became fascinated by—almost obsessed with—the role of human beings in the metaphysical structure of the universe. Particularly in *Nightwood* and *The Antiphon*, one readily can observe her preoccupation with a metaphysical structure that bears resemblances to the Great Chain of Being, the structure, reified in the eighteenth century, in which man is positioned between salvation and damnation, is caught halfway between the angels and the beasts. In Barnes' late writings characters are positioned along a spectrum of their relationship to these two extremes. Kenneth Burke's linguistic analysis of Barnes' *Nightwood* hints that Barnes represents her characters in that work, for example, through verbal constructions which reveal the posturings of their bodies in conjunction with their metaphysical conditions: through "standing," "bending," "bowing," "crouching," "kneeling," and "lying."[1] Although such images often appear

---

[1]Kenneth Burke, "Version, Con-, Per, and In- (Thoughts on Djuna

in these early tales (in "The Coward" Varra is characterized as positioning herself in bed "furtively, with a crouching movement"; the wife of Pilaat in "The Terrorists" is described as wearing heavy boots "that seemed to be drawing her down."), in 1916 Barnes had not yet developed such conceits fully. It is apparent in this early work, nonetheless, that Barnes' disinterest in particularized character and her emphasis on action point to the later preoccupation with moral conditions.

Each of Barnes' approaches to character, voice, and plot, in fact, reinforce one another in pushing her tales toward abstraction. A highly stereotyped character inevitably must be presented as acting in a more exaggerated, theatrical manner; and an authorial focus on action more clearly reveals character behavior, which, in turn, profiles the type. Barnes' persistent intrusions and her oracular statements can be understood, moreover, as drawing character away from the particular, as an attempt to generalize the specific. And, ultimately, such a conjunction of techniques directs these tales toward a revelation of moral values. Witnessing man become type through action, the reader is encouraged to place and judge Barnes' figures. And in that context, the catchwords of these early stories—"freedom," "cowardice," "terror," "sensitivity," and "beauty"—suddenly take on new meaning.

Barnes Novel *Nightwood*)," in his *Language as Symbolic Action: Essays on Life, Literature, and Method* (Berkeley: University of California Press, 1968), pp. 240-253.

In the light of Barnes' interest in these values in a time of increasing moral relativity, it becomes evident why Barnes never adapted much to the Modernist way of thinking and writing of life. In relation to the literature of her close friends, T. S. Eliot and James Joyce, Barnes' writing may always appear as an anomaly. This early fiction, accordingly, cannot be properly evaluated by Modern " normative realist" standards. Barnes' is a private vision, a moralistic vision that is perhaps more at home in our own time, when fiction writing has been increasingly influenced by moral satirists such as Donald Barthelme, Steve Katz, Harry Matthews, Russell Banks, and Gilbert Sorrentino. And although Barnes' early tales are not major works of literature—Barnes, herself, has dismissed them as juvenilia[1]—they are important, I believe, in the context of our current literary concerns. Perhaps today, more than any period since their first appearance, we can readily share the pleasures of these short tales.

Douglas Messerli
Temple University

---

[1]Djuna Barnes, in an interview with the author on November 26, 1973.

Smoke

and Other Early Stories

Contents

The Terrible Peacock

I t was during the dull season, when a subway accident looms as big as a Thaw getaway, that an unusual item was found loose in the coffee.

Nobody seemed to know whence it had come. It dealt with a woman, one greater, more dangerous than Cleopatra, thirty-nine times as alluring as sunlight on a gold eagle, and about as elusive.

She was a Peacock, said the item, which was not ill-written—a slinky female with electrifying green eyes and red hair, dressed in clinging green-and-blue-silk, and she was very much observed as she moved languorously through the streets of Brooklyn. A Somebody—but who?

The city editor scratched his head and gave the item to Karl. "Find out about her," he suggested.

"Better put a new guy on," said Karl. "Get the fresh angle. I got that Kinney case to look after today. What about Garvey?"

"All right," said the city editor, and selected a fresh piece of gum.

Garvey was duly impressed when Karl hove to alongside his desk and flung his leg after the item onto it, for Karl was the Star.

Rather a mysterious person in a way, was Karl. His residence was an inviolable secret. He was known to have accumulated money, despite the fact that he was a newspaperman. It was also known that he had married.

Otherwise, he was an emergency man—a first-rate reporter. When someone thought best to commit suicide and leave a little malicious note to a wife who raved three steps into the bathroom and three into the kitchen, hiccuping "Oh, my God!" with each step, it got into Karl's typewriter—and there was the birth of a front-page story.

"So you're to look her up," said Karl. "She's dashed beautiful, has cat eyes and Leslie Carter hair—a loose-jointed, ball-brearing Clytie, rigged out with a complexion like creamed coffee stood overnight. They say she claws more men into her hair than any siren living or dead."

"You've seen her?" breathed Garvey, staring.

Karl nodded briefly.

"Why don't *you* get her, then?"

"There are two things," said Karl judicially, "at which I am no good. One is subtraction, and the other is attraction. Go to it, son. The assignment is yours."

He strolled away, but not too late to see Garvey swelling visibly at the implied compliment and caressing his beautiful, lyric tie.

Garvey didn't altogether like the assignment, nonetheless. There was Lilac Jane, you see. He had a date with her for that very night, and Lilac Jane was exceedingly desirable.

He was at that age when devotion to one female of the species makes dalliance with any others nothing short of treason.

But—he had been allotted this work because of his fascinations for slinky green sirens! Garvey fingered the tie again and withdrew his lavender scented handkerchief airily, as an alterboy swings a censer.

At the door he turned under the light and pushed back his

cuff, and his fellow workers groaned. It was seven by his wristwatch

Outside he paused on the corner near the chophouse. He looked up and down the gloomy street with its wilted florist-window displays and its spattering of gray house fronts, wishing there were someone with him who could be told of his feeling of competence in a world of competent men.

His eyes on the pavement, lost in perfervid dreams of Lilac Jane, he wandered on. The roaring of the bridge traffic disturbed him not, nor the shouts of bargemen through the dusk on the waterfront.

At last through the roseate visions loomed something green.

Shoes! Tiny shoes, trim and immaculate; above them a glimpse of thin, green stockings on trimmer ankles.

There was a tinkle of laughter, and Garvey came to himself, red and perspiring, and raised his eyes past the slim, green-clad body to the eyes of the Peacock.

It was she beyond question. Her hair was terribly red, even in the darkness, and it gleamed a full eight inches above her forehead, piled higher than any hair Garvey had ever seen. The moon shone through it like butter through mosquito netting.

Her neck was long and white, her lipes were redder than her hair, and her green eyes, with the close-fitting, silken dress, that undulated like troubled, weed-filled water as she moved, completed the whole daring creation. The powers that be had gone in for poster effects when they made the Peacock.

She was handsome beyond belief, and she was amused at Garvey. Her silvery laugh tinkled out again as he stared at her, his pulse a hundred in the shade.

He tried to convince himself that this physiological effect was due to his newspaper instinct, but it is to be conjectured that Lilac Jane would have had her opinion of the Peacock had she been present.

"Well, young man?" she demanded, the wonderful eyes getting in their deadly work.

"I—I'm sorry—I didn't mean—" Garvey floundered hopelessly, but he did not try to escape.

"You were handing me bouquets by staring like that? That what you're trying to say?"

She laughed again, glided up to him and took his arm. "I like you, young man," she said.

"My nun-name is Garvey, and I'm on the—the *Argus.*"

She started at that and looked at him sharply. "A reporter!"

But her tinkly laugh rang out again, and they walked on. "Well, why not?" she said gaily.

Then, with entire unexpectedness: "Do you tango?"

Garvey nodded dumbly, struggling to find his tongue.

"I *love* it!" declared the Peacock, taking a step or two of the dance beside him. "Want to take me somewheres so we can have a turn or two?"

Garvey swallowed hard and mentioned a well-known resort.

"Mercy!" cried the green-eyed siren, turning shocked orbs upon him. "I don't drink! Let's go to a tearoom—Poiret's." She called it "Poyrett's."

Garvey suffered himself to be led to the slaughter, and as they went she chattered lightly. He drew out his handkerchief and dabbed gently at his temples.

"Gracious!" she drawled. "You smell like an epidemic of

swooning women."

Garvey was hurt, but deep within himself he decided suddenly that scent was out of place on a masculine cold-assuager.

They turned into a brightly lighted establishment where there were already a few girls and fewer men.

They found a table, and she ordered some tea and cakes, pressing her escort not to be bashful as far as himself was concerned. Garvey ordered obediently and lavishly.

Presently the music struck up, and he swung her out on the floor and into the fascinating dance.

Now, Garvey was really some dancer. But the Peacock!

She was light and sinuous as a wreath of green mist, yet solid bone and muscle in his arms.

She was the very poetry of motion, the spirit of the dance, the essence of grace and beauty.

And when the music stopped, Garvey could have cried with vexation, though he was considerably winded.

But the Peacock was not troubled at all. Indeed, she had talked on through all the dance.

Garvey had capitulated long ago. Lilac Jane? Bah! What were a thousand Lilac Janes to this glorious creature, this Venus Anadyomene—Aphrodite of the Sea-Foam?

In the bright light of the tearoom her green eyes were greener, her red hair redder, her white throat whiter. He would have given a Texas ranch for her, with the cattle thrown in.

He tried to tell her something of this, and she laughed delightfully.

"What is it about me that makes men go mad over me?" she demanded, dreamily sipping her tea.

"Do they?" He winced.

"Oh, shamelessly. They drop their jaws, propriety, and any bundles they may be carrying. Why?"

"It's the most natural thing in the world. You have hair and eyes that few women have, and a man desires the rare." He was getting eloquent.

"But—I'm not at all pretty—thinness isn't attractive, is it?"

"It is, in you," he said simply. The fact that he could say it simply was very bad indeed for Lilac Jane.

She dimpled at him and arose abruptly. "Now I've got to vanish. Oh, Lily!"

A girl, undeniably pretty, but just an ordinary girl, crossed over.

"This is Mr.—er—Garvey, Miss Jones. Keep him amused, will you? He dances very nicely." And as he struggled to his feet, attempting a protest: "Oh, I'm coming back again," and she was gone.

Garvey tried to think of some excuse to escape from the partner thus unceremoniously thrust upon him, but the girl blocked his feeble efforts by rising expectantly as the strains of "Too Much Mustard" floated on the ambient atmosphere.

There was nothing for it but to make good. And, after all, she was a nice dancer. He found himself asking what she would have at the end of the dance.

Anyhow, he reflected, he had still his assignment to cover. The Peacock was still as great a mystery as ever—more of a mystery. But she had said that she would return. So he waited and danced and ate and treated.

Half an hour later the Peacock *did* return—with another man.

To Garvey everything turned suddenly light purple. That

was the result of his being green with jealousy and seeing red at the same time.

The newest victim of her lures (for such even Garvey recognized him to be) was an elderly business man, inclined to corpulency, with a free and roving eye. Garvey hated him with a bitter hatred.

The Peacock danced once with him, then abandoned him, gasping fishily, to another girl's tender mercies.

She stopped briefly at Garvey's table, gave him a smile and a whispered: "Here, tomorrow night," and vanished in a swirl of green silk—probably in search of more captives.

Garvey put in a bad night and a worse next day. Who was she? What was her little game? What would happen tomorrow night?

He didn't care. Lilac Jane was definitely deposed in favor of a green goddess whose lure quite possibly spelled destruction.

But he didn't care.

He told the city editor that the Peacock story would be available next day, and added the mental reservation, "if I haven't resigned." And he mooned through the work in a trance that made for serious errors in his "copy."

Yet he had no illusions about it, save an undefined and noble impulse to "rescue the Peacock from her degrading surroundings."

Somehow the phrase didn't quite apply, though.

Once he thought of Lilac Jane, with her warm, normal, womanly arms stretched out to him. He took her picture from his pocket and compared it with the mental picture he carried of the Peacock, then put the photograph back, face outward.

Thus Lilac Jane's flags were struck.

Directly afterward the brazen office-boy communicated to him in strident tones that a "skoit" wanted him on the phone.

For a second he thought of the Peacock; but no, Lilac Jane was due to call. Whereupon he fled ignominiously.

It may be deduced that he had not forgotten Lilac Jane after all, merely misplaced her.

Garvey fell into the elevator, the cosmic tail of the Peacock filling his existence. He threw quoits with the god of a greater wisdom, and came out of his reverie and the elevator with a pair of jet earrings dancing before him. They were the earrings of Lilac Jane.

But beneath them, as the periods beneath double exclamation points, floated a pair of green boots.

Moodily he ate, moodily he went to his room—apartment, I beg his pardon. And at six o'clock he was ready for eight.

He took out his watch and wound it until the hands quivered and it made noises inside as though it were in pain.

He stood before the mirror and motioned at his Adam's apple, prodding the lyric tie into shape and stretching his neck the while until it seemed about to snap and leave a blank space between his chin and his collar button.

A man in love ceases mentally. All his energy is devoted to his outward appearance.

If Napoleon had been in love while on the field of Austerlitz, he would not have rejoiced in his heart, but in his surtout and small clothes.

If Wellington had been so afflicted during the battle of Waterloo, the result might have been different.

Therefore, when Garvey was finally attired, he was like unto the lilies of the field that toil not, neither do they spin. He glanced at his watch when all was at last perfect, and all but sat down suddenly. It was midnight!

But then he saw that the poor watch was travelling at the rate of a mile a minute, trying to make up for that last winding. The alarm clock said seven-thirty.

Whereupon Garvey achieved the somewhat difficult feat of descending the stairs without bending his knees. Spoil the crease in his trousers? Never!

And shortly thereafter he was at the tango tearoom, looking around eagerly for the Peacock, his heart pounding harder than his watch.

The place was crowded, and the dancers were already busy to the sprightly strains of "Stop at Chattanooga."

For a space he looked in vain. Then his cardiac engine missed a stroke.

There she was—seated at a table in the far corner.

As fast as he reasonably could without danger to his immaculateness, Garvey headed Her-ward.

Yes, it was undoubtedly the Peacock. She was leaning her elbows on the table and talking earnestly—talking to—Karl!

Garvey was abreast of the table by now. He must have made some sort of a noise, for they both looked up.

The Peacock smiled sweetly, with a touch of defiance. Karl grinned amiably, with a touch of sheepishness. And both said: "Hello!"

Then said Karl: "Old man, allow me to present you to—my wife."

Garvey choked and sat down speechless.

"Might as well 'fess it," said Karl. "Only please remember that the idea was solely mine."

"It was *not*!" said the Peacock sharply. "You wouldn't *hear*

33

of it when I suggested it."

"Well, anyhow, I have all my money invested in this tearoom. But business has been mighty dull; it looked like bankruptcy.

"Then Mrs. Karl here—she was La Dancerita before she fell for me, you see, and—well, she's been drumming up patronage."

"It was fun!" declared La Dancerita-that-was. "I nearly got pinched once, though."

"I wrote that squib at the office that got you the assignment, thinking to help the game along a little." He smiled a deep, mahogany, wrinkled smile that disarmed when it reached the blue of his eyes. "So now you know all about the Peacock."

Garvey swallowed twice and sighed once. Then he took something from his breast pocket and put it back again.

"I—er know somebody that likes to tango," he said irrelevantly.

Paprika Johnson

E very Saturday, just as soon as she had slipped her manilla pay envelope down her neck, had done up her handkerchiefs and watered the geraniums, Paprika Johnson climbed onto the fire-escape and reached across the strings of her pawnshop banjo.

Paprika Johnson played softly, and she sang softly too, from a pepsin disinfected throat, and more than reverently she scattered the upper register into the flapping white wash of the O'Briens.

Sitting there in the dusk, upon her little square of safety, in a city of a million squares, she listened to the music of the spheres and the frying of the onions in Daisy Mack's back kitchen, and she sang a song to flawless summer, while she watched Madge Darsey loosen her stays in the tenement house opposite.

Below Paprika, straight as a plumb-bob would direct, sat the patrons of Swingerhoger's Beer Garden, at small brown tables that had once been green, perhaps, or blue. Paprika, unconscious of the laws of state, the rules of Sanskrit, and of the third dimensions, was also unaware of the trade that waged below her; was unaware of the hoisting of hops and of dilettanteism.

Also, in the beginning, she was unaware of the existence of the boy from Stroud's. This is beginning at the beginning.

Paprika had a bosom friend, in the days when roses found

no hedge from her neck to her hair, when she allotted to them no design, save the generous and gentle smiling bow that was her mouth. And her bosom friend, like all bosom things, was necessary and uncomfortable.

She borrowed incessantly, did Leah, she borrowed Paprika's slippers out of bed, and her shifts into bed, and she borrowed her face powder, and her hair ribbons and her stockings. And she borrowed, most of all, Paprika's charm.

Leah was thin and pock-marked and colorless, and still, without the stiffness of a wall flower was one, and chose Gus to lean on.

It goes without saying that Gustav was blind, as blind as a man in a rage and as a man in love.

He listened to Paprika's soft voice, and not being able to estimate the distance that sound carries, put his arm about Leah's waist while Paprika sat upon the other side of the table.

Leah would have been just as well pleased to have had Gus in her own room, but that was impossible, as it was chaperonless.

Paprika was safe, because Paprika had a moribund mother under the counterpane, a chaperone who never spoke or moved, since she was paralyzed, but who was a pretty good one at that, being a white exclamation point this side of error. Therefore, Leah was hugged in Paprika's presence.

Gus thought he knew what he was doing, because on his trip to the back sink in the hall, he heard things about Paprika that were kind and good to listen to, and he thought they were said of the one he hugged. Therefore, he shaved and was happy.

Now, listen; I'll tell you something.

Gustav kept behind his ninety-eight-cent alarm clock,

where he could not lose it, the address of an oculist who would cure him for a remuneration. No one is sending perfect cattle to heaven without pocket padding, so Gus waited until he could pay to see again, and in the meantime, toiled up to the eighth floor of evenings and sat with the girls. And Paprika being a bosom friend worth having, lent Leah her violet extract.

At night when she dug into bed, Paprika exchanged notes with Leah about their mutual work. Paprika typewrote and Leah pushed Sloe Gin Fizz toward erring youths, who drank with averted faces.

Which proves without my saying it, that Leah was all right on the inside—perhaps—but that her intentions were a lot better than her claims on beauty.

Yet, Leah realized and gave worship for the part that Paprika had played for her, she comprehended, and was almost humble by the devotion of her friend, in keeping Gus's arms about her waist. She whispered her loyalty into Paprika's ear in the silence of the night, while Paprika pushed her gum into the leg of the bed.

Among other things, Leah said that she would do as much for her sometime, in another way—if she could, and lay back, knowing that the dark was doing as much for her as it was for the hole in the carpet.

Paprika was touched and bought a banjo.

So on evenings when she had talked Gustav's arm half way round Leah's waist, she took her banjo out upon the fire escape, and practiced a complicated movement from Chopin.

Across the cliff she looked and watched the moon grope its way up the sky and over condensed milk signs and climb to the top of the Woolworth Building. And Paprika wondered if her time was soon coming and smiled, for she knew that she was as good to look upon as a yard of slick taffy, and twice as alluring.

Unconsciously, Paprika was the cabaret performer of the beer garden. The men about the tables put their hands into their shirt bosoms, and felt the ticking of the tolerably good clock their mother had given them. Or others felt into the breast pockets and felt the syncopated beat of the watch their father had given them (from frequenting just such a garden). And others, without any inherited momentum, looked wanly upon the open faces of dollar Ingersols, and sipped with slow, bated breath.

The combination of Paprika, beer and the moon got into the street and nudged the boy off his stool at the head of Stroud's donkeys stabled in lower Bleecker Street; edged him off, and after a while it was said that the boy from Stroud's was becoming a man in Swingerhoger's beer garden.

The boy from Stroud's was a tall blond wimpet who had put his hands into his mother's hair and shaken it free of gold; a lad who had painted his cheeks from the palette of the tenderloin, the pink that descends from one member of a family to the other, quicksilver running down life's page. And the fact that at twenty the boy from Stroud's still had it, proved that he was his mother's only child. He also had great gray eyes, and an impassible mouth, a hand that was made for soft-brimmed hats and love notes, and a breaking voice like a ferryboat coming in from Staten Island.

He sat in the beer garden three nights before he dared follow up the music from above. When he looked, he decided that the perspective on Paprika made her very alluring. And so the boy from Stroud's, who had turned the donkeys around for supper, crowded down, into the portfolio of his soul, the pattern of P. Johnson.

And she, all oblivious and smelling of white roses and talcum, might have gone on indefinitely, but one night, stumbling up the stairs in the dark, came against a little packet. She picked it up and, woman-like, tried to read it in the hall. Failing, and being over-anxious to discover its contents, she tried again at the crack of light running along Daisy Mack's door, and on to the fifth floor, running up a little higher and balancing herself vertically over a vertical package at Eliza Farthingale's. But Eliza burned only one candle, and Paprika could make less of it than ever, and finally, having got to her room by a long stage of short runs, read it in the light from her open door, saw that the hand was a masculine one. And being Paprika and a woman, and thinking that she had nothing on her bosom friend, she sidled in backward and dropped it in among the bananas on the sideboard.

After supper she took it and the banjo out upon the fire-escape, and read it by the light of the moon.

The involuntary suicides in the beer garden sipped slowly and finally ceased altogether, and Swingerhoger, who had hopes of rolling up silk sleeves out of them, became uneasy at the sight of bricklayers whining over their brew. He did not know that all the trouble came of a silent banjo. Paprika wasn't playing, she was reading the note from the boy. Inside the note was a photograph taken side face with a soft look and collar; his fine Roman nose was enchanced by a dark background. What did it matter to her if he was turning the donkey around?

About this time, when Leah, who had lost part control of her hands, never being sure when she could use them—lost control of her one finger on the left hand altogether, it being weighed down by the weight of a diamond, purchased by Gus.

Paprika kissed her, and Leah went down upon her knees and thanked God for a willing sacrifice, and, by way of surety, prayed that Gus might remain forever in the dark. Then arising, she dusted her knees and inquired of Paprika if she looked well in curlpapers, and got into bed.

"My dear," said Paprika, wiggling her toes in the last effort to get comfortable, "Don't let him know anything about it— ever—me, I mean. And if, after you are married I can do anything, just whoop and I'll be there. By the way, are you going to start in, in Yonkers, where they have Gaby Deslys and cats, or in the Bronx, where you get commuter's grouch and new laid eggs?"

Leah answered from the depths of the bed and Paprika's warm arm. "Neither. You see, dear, Gus is a sort of cousin to Mr. Swingerhoger, and Swingerhoger is going to let Gus run a part of the business, and pay him a salary, and so we are not going to leave you, only to move in downstairs, into the second floor front. And I'm so glad."

"Why?" demanded Paprika, losing forever the vision and the hope of the second floor front.

"Because I'll be near you, dear—don't you understand?"

And Paprika, being a good bosom friend, understood.

Now, the boy from Stroud's, having gotten tired of picking straw out of the donkey's ears, decided to take a risk and pick a wife out of the sky.

He had seen Paprika from the beer garden, but Paprika was eight floors distant, and though his soul's eyes were extra keen, they were not keen enough to discover, with any directly satisfying accuracy, whether Paprika's petticoats were three or two, as he got her, a silhouette aginst Manhattan, enchanted keen, they were not keen enough to discover, with any direct-ly satisfying accuracy, whether Paprika's petticoats were three or two, as he got her, a silhouette against Manhattan, enhanced as she was by the whole of the left side of the Hudson, he came to the conclusion that she was fit for a flat off Bleecker Street with eggs for breakfast.

And so it was that Paprika presently bought a yard of baby blue ribbon and tied up a bunch of letters and put them beneath her chemises in the lower drawer.

She did not think that she was taking a risk. She had seen the picture of the boy, and he was a good cameo, so she allowed her heart to keep pace with him, as Dan Patch with his shadow. In her mind's eye she was already carrying the shaving soap into the dressing room.

In a flurry of hot ginger tea and white voile, Leah was married. For the last time, a single girl, without as yet the knowledge of the one-sided effect of a dresser with military brushes on one corner, and an automatic stop on the other. She hugged and kissed Paprika and cried a lot down her neck and felt that she was being parted by the whole of a geography and an isthmus. And after they carried her Swedish trunk and her bouquet down to the second floor front and she and Gus turned at the landing and threw kisses back to Paprika, who leaned over the banister.

Paprika hitched up her one-fifty "American Madame," patted her back hair and went and sat down upon the china chest.

She was grateful to circumstances that had made it possible to swap the boy for Leah. Also she sang as she played her banjo, and didn't care that the night got in front of the Municipal tower and shut out the million lights.

But the man in the beer garden, who was nobody in particular, spoke to Swingerhoger.

"Why haven't you discovered for yourself that the drawing card here is that little girl who comes in about three beer time, and after pinning her handkerchiefs to the sash, yanks the strings of the banjo into the harmony of the human breast?"

Swingerhoger made a warp of his fingers to catch the woof of his gold seals, and looked worried.

"Are you perfectly sure that they come here to hear her play as much as for anything?"

"As much as for anything," answered the man, who was nobody in particular. "They think they have found the spring and the song, which has left the city altogether, and the cry of the birds and the plaint of a woman, the rarest things I know in little old New York."

"Perhaps you're right," said Swingerhoger. "Perhaps if I put it to her delicately, she will take it in the right way, which is, that it is a compliment and an honor to play to Swingerhoger guests, and she may put in more of her time at it."

The man who was nobody in particular looked a long while into the inherited vapid face of the garden owner, and he did not think of the arrangement of that gentleman's mind.

"You must pay her," he said.

"Pay her? What for?"

"To play and sing, my friend. She has a job somewhere in this lonesome city, and she must fill the hours. If you pay her she can play for you from, say, four to twelve p.m., and then you are already a wealthy man."

"But," said Swingerhoger, dropping his seals, "no other

beer garden is doing this."

"And that," said the man who was nobody in particular, "is where you get in your start. When the thing gets winded all the gardens will take it up, and then you're done. But until then the chance is yours."

To Paprika, therefore, Swingerhoger took the proposition.

The man from nowhere, who was nobody in particular, got a free beer.

"Play for you?" queried Paprika, keeping him out by the chain on the door. "How can I? I have a stenographer's job to fill, in a silk office. I'm getting ten per, and it just keeps tapioca in mother's mouth and the pepsin in mine, and it hangs out a few starched things and a ride now and then on the cars."

"You don't understand. I pay you ten dollars just the same and all you got to do is lie in bed all day until four and then you play for me until midnight and hit the mattress again, see?"

"Gee!" gasped Paprika, "in bed all day. I'm dreamin', but say, I can't do it anyway, because," she blushed this time, "I'm leaving soon." She smiled, the last letter from the boy lay next her fifth rib.

"But," he protested, walking down backward, as she followed, "you don't understand. Nothing to do all day and then only play an easy tune now and again, between bites of the pralines and sips at the sherry lemonade. I'm getting rich on you, Miss Johnson. Think it over. Why, only today I gave my cousin Gus a bank account on you."

Paprika smiled again and shook her head. "I'm changing my tune anyway," she said, and added softly, "to a lullaby."

And so at last, though she had never seen the boy from Stroud's face to face, she put the chair over the rent in the carpet, the vase over the moth hole in the piano scarf, and the stain just back of the hat rack she covered with a picture of three pink gowned girls walking over a brittle paper stream.

Her heart beat terribly fast. She got that same sensation that Leah had gotten. She felt that nothing was going to be as it had been. She took a dose of soda water, but it was not the treatment for the trouble. Therefore, resigning herself to her best dress and a peach of a haircomb, she waited for the boy from Stroud's who was coming to see her.

The little hands on the clock came coquettishly in front of its gold face and parted suddenly as if saying, "Oh, all's well, I need not hide," with the pettish nonchalance of ninety-eight cent clocks.

Paprika fussed a bit with the position of her feet and decided, after all, that she looked better standing up, and had gotten a pose to suit every one, herself included, half drooping over moth-eaten geraniums, when Leah hurled herself into the room.

"Oh, my God!" she said, stumbling over to the mantlepiece, and stood there shaking.

"He got it from behind the clock," she wailed, "and now the oculists have taken their last diagnosis, and they say that he can have the bandage removed, and I didn't understand and I'm done, I'm done." She took to shaking the mantle and its blue array of willowware and the peacock feathers sticking in the mucilage. Also she shook Paprika.

"What can I do?" asked Paprika, and Leah fell upon her.

"This once—this once—he would never get over the shock—and I can't, I can't!"

"You can't what?" demanded Paprika.

"It's Gus, you don't understand. The oculists have just left him and he can *see!*"

"*Well?*"

Leah took a step toward the girl who had been her bosom friend, and she heaved her forty-nine-cent belt up. "He mustn't see me—yet."

And so she stood. Leah, the friend who had got a husband in the dark, and now must stand before him in the light that had come to him with his prosperity, gotten by the playing of Paprika. And Paprika, realizing this, did not know what to do.

Leah came to her and took her arms in both her hands, nursing them between her palms with long frightened fingers, and looked at Paprika and could not speak.

Paprika had forgotten the boy from Stroud's. She had forgotten her best dress and the sense of back thrust feet, and she put her chin out.

"You want him to pin his eyes on *me?*"

And Leah nodded her thin head back and forth, and took her lip in between her teeth. "He won't be so sorry, after— when he gets used to it and me, when I come in later and you straighten things out. He will be too much a man to be a quitter."

And Paprika understood what it meant to a woman to be willing to keep her own at such a cost. Also Paprika thought she was over-estimating Gus's sense of beauty.

So she said "all right," looked at the clock and thought, at a rough estimate, that she had time, and descended to the second floor front.

She stirred as she sat by Gus's bed at the step on the stair that halted a bit, and then went on up. She remembered that she had told nothing to Leah about his coming, and Leah was up there in the dusk—but Gus was taking the bandages off.

In the dim light, the boy from Stroud's took off his hat. He was breathing hard from the eight flights and a heart full of a sensation that was like being run over with molasses and crowned with chocolate meringue. In the corner he saw the dim shape of a woman. He never looked toward the bed where slept the perfect chaperon. He shut the door reverently and came a step in. The figure in the corner moved and moaned like a seal at twelve p.m., moved and moaned and put her hand to her unlovely hair and blinked at him from, startled blue eyes with her mouth open.

The banjo leaning in the corner caught his eye as he leaned forward, and he laughed suddenly, shortly, with a hard disillusioned break, and suddenly, without a word, caught up his hat and ran pantingly down the stairs. Heedless, he ran past the second story front on to the first, and fell into the murky light of Swingerhoger's beer garden, threw up his hands and cried something about "perspective and a picture plane" and darted out of the garden and disappeared in the direction of Bleecker Street.

Well, that's about all, excepting as we said, Paprika Johnson still holds the job as the first cabaret artist, at thirty years old. Still of evenings she sits upon the fire-escape and plays her banjo as her handkerchiefs dry, just as she did on that afternoon three minutes after Gus had taken the bandages off and she had come into the garden to get a pitcher of lemonade to celebrate, and leaning across the counter, she had said, "All right, I'll take that job."

Also she never told Leah that her chance "to do as much for her sometime, in a different way," had come and gone.

What Do You See, Madam?

Mamie Saloam was a dancer.

She had come from the lower stratum of the poor, who drape their shoulders with cotton, and their stomachs with gingham.

The Bowery, which is no place at all for virtue or duplicity, had seen Mamie try on her first fit of sulks and her first stay laces. They knew then that her pattern was Juno, her heritage Joseph, and her ambition jade. At the age of ten she had learned to interpret Oscar Wilde, when Oscar Wilde had gone in, rather extensively, for passion and the platter, and had paried off creation with a movement and a beard.

On that moonlit night, when she chucked Semco, the sailor, under the chin, and swiped one of the park lilacs for keeps, Mamie grew up.

Between his lips and hers she had learned competition. His was the greater kiss, his arms the greater strength, his voice the master voice.

Mamie became fire and felt hell where it burns low among the coals, and the street that sensed her homecoming on staccato heels, heard the wide-mouthed laughter she threw her mother as she rolled into bed.

Thereafter she swore that her life should be given to portraying detached emotions, to placing love on the boards.

Her ambition was to kiss the lips of John the Baptist as they lay in plaster glory upon a little tin plate.

When a subaltern puts his head under cover, he is a coward. When Mamie Saloam sought the underside of the counterpane she was merely looking for future ethics.

Mamie twisted the Bowery out of her hair, threw her hips into the maelstrom of rightly moving things, and raised an organism of potato and cod to the level of caviar and champagne. When she turned about, she had taken three steps in the direction of the proverbial gentleman who follows after the world and the flesh.

The rich and the poor are divided only in the matter of scorn, eye scorn, lip scorn, and the sudden rude laughter that runs the gamut of Broadway. All these leaped into Mamie's saucy face as she looked at herself for the first time in a mirror that gave her back, whole.

When she walked out, one heard only the sound of slum slippers and the regular cadence of her knees as she descended the steps. She was used to uneven footing.

After the mirror she swore that she had taken the last cod bone from between her teeth and now she would chew only after-dinner mints.

When a girl gives up gum and alleys, and has known little else, she becomes something different, and the something different that Mamie became was a dancer, toe and otherwise.

Into the little world of the painted came Mamie. Into that place of press-agents and powder-puffs, of Lillian Russell and Raymond Hitchcock, of Irving and of Sarah, scented with lilac and Bel Bon, throbbing and pulsating with the sound of laughter; into that little stall called the dressing room, out of which none may come unchanged.

What Do You See, Madam?

Mamie Saloam was a good medium on which to lay cosmetics. Everything merely accentuated those points that God and the Saloams had given her; in fact, the teamwork between the two had been sublime. Mamie was beautiful.

She was loved by the men down front because she had mastered the technique of the tights.

Her world held rows and rows of dusty caned chairs, and over these, like migrating robins, the pink anatomy of the chorus—hips thrown out against the painted drop, listless eyes that saw only supper, a new step, and once in awhile, some other things. Mamie Saloam could go where she willed. She could stoop or look up because Mamie breathed true ambition and heroic drudgery.

When she passed the boundaries of decency it was a full run for your money; when she went up in smoke, those original little pasty pans of Egypt became chimney pots. If Helen of Troy could have been seen eating peppermints out of a paper bag, it is highly probable that her admirers would have been an entirely different class.

It is the thing you are found doing while the horde looks on that you shall be loved for—or ignored.

Billy had caught Mamie pinning "Thou shalt not sin" up high on the door of her room in the house of chameleon thoughts. He then knew—for even electricians can know things—that the way to approach Mamie was to sit close and abide in hope, for opportunity comes once to every man.

While he waited, Mamie made up her one philosophy. It was made, of course, for the benefit of women. It read: "A woman never knows what she sees, therefore, she tries to see what she knows."

"Listen," said the stage manager one night from out of the

gloom where Mamie sat restringing the beads that passed for combinations, underskirt, shift petticoat, bodice skirt, and withal, propriety for Salome. "Listen, we are in a fix. The P.I.B. is on to us and you."

"In what way?" inquired Mamie Saloam.

"They have gotten on to the fact that early in the season we are to present you as *Salome*. They have prejudices—"

"Of course they have," said Mamie calmly; "they have seen Mme. Aguglia, Mary Garden, Gertrude Hoffman, and Trixie Friganza do the stunt; they have all seen what they wanted to see because the aforesaid showed them what they wanted to see. I'll admit that John hasn't been properly loved since the original gurgle ceased; I'll admit that as we have gotten further and further away from the real head, we have dealt with rather papier-mache passions.

"John was rather lethargic in his response even in the beginning, and we have made too much fuss over him. When a man is dead, a certain respect is due him; it is a proper and a joyous thing to dance about him, but I do think he has been rather overkissed. I will show the ladies of the P.I.B. the necessary moderation, even if the gentleman is helpless. Leave it to me."

"By the way," she added as the stage manager pondered, his hand in his hair, "what is the P.I.B.?"

"It is the Prevention of Impurities upon the Boards," he said, and smiled at her.

"And what do they want?"

"They either want the performance stopped or—they want to see a purely impartial rendering."

Billy looked at her from beneath his shaggy eyebrows. Then suddenly he let go of the thing that is called reserve and took her hand.

"Mamie," he said, "couldn't you respond to me; couldn't I ever be anything to you; couldn't I make up for all this"—he waved his arm broadcast—"this ambition stuff?"

"Billy," she said, and her voice was cold and practical, "I couldn't ever boil potatoes over the heat of your affection. Your love would never bridge a gap; it wouldn't even fill up the hole that the mice came through, and," she concluded, withdrawing her hand, "I couldn't ever consider anyone less than John."

Deep down in Billy's heart lay a terrible passion that itched to force this allegorical obstacle from between him and the woman. As he sat in his perch up in the wings and focused the blue light upon the platter and the white upturned plaster face, he knew what had put the word "La mort" into the dictionary and into circulation, and he groaned within his soul.

The next day they took away the dusty rows of chairs, the heaps of discarded tights, shed by human butterflies that had grown into something more brilliant or had died emerging from the chrysalis prematurely. They did not notice that it was dusty until they saw two spots some three inches apart, which looked as if someone had been upon his knees.

They did not speculate any further, but Mamie saw.

The stage hands cleaned and fussed in preparation for the trial scene to be given for the benefit of the P.I.B. A pitcher, belonging to the dresser, very much cracked, and yet gaudy as the owner, was filled with lemonade, which first frosted the outside like a young woman's demeanor when holding the young man off, and finally broke out into great beads and slid over the hips of the pitcher to the table below like the tears that follow up the first grief.

It was quite dark back stage when they were through. The little bags of ballast that let down Florida or France from the ceiling hung swaying fifty feet above Billy as he tinkered with the lights.

Out front sat the stage manager between the starched ladies of the P.I.B., drinking the lemonade gently yet firmly from tall, frail glasses. They looked at each other across the chain-encircled vest of the stage manager with the macaw look which is strictly limited to boards of prevention and committees for inspection.

They would like to think well of Mamie Saloam, but as Mamie said, they had seen Mme. Aguglia.

Then out across the dusky stage came Mamie, tall and dominating. Her bare shoulders supported vivid streams of her hair.

For a minute she stood poised in the center of the stage, a voluptuous outline in the mist.

Then the spotlight fell, not upon Mamie, but upon the face of John, upturned and white, with half-closed lids, the hair and beard flowing over the edge of the plate. Dark loops broke the dead white of the forehead, a silent questioning of the painted lips awaiting the performance of Mamie Saloam, who had learned to kiss ten years before.

The ladies of the P.I.B, not to be fooled, leaned sternly over their glasses. They wanted to be sure that there was a simplicity in the way Mamie Saloam wallowed before her lord.

On she came, halting, and then suddenly broke into a semicircle of half-steps about the head of the dead Baptist, gurgling, throaty little noises escaping her lips. Slowly she lowered herself until, imperceptibly to the starched ladies, she lay upon the floor and sinuously wriggled toward the tin platter.

Sidewise, forward, approaching it with plastic hands, nearer and nearer and nearer till the platter was within the zone of her very breath. Over it she hovered, murmuring, while her eyes changed from blue to green and from green to deep opal. Then suddenly she dropped her chin among the strands of the flowing beard.

The starched ladies sighed and relaxed. Here was a woman at last who could do the thing with perfect impartiality. They turned approving eyes upon the manager.

"She has John under perfect control," they said, and passed out.

Then Mamie did a strange thing. She sat up, put her arms about her knees, and looked serenely at the face still motionless in the blue of the light from the unoccupied electrician's box. John the Baptist batted his right eye.

"Get up, Billy," she said. "It's all right. Let us thank the dark of a back stage night, and your ability to lie still. At last I have proved that a woman never knows what she is seeing."

Who Is This Tom Scarlett?

He snarls.

It is a philosophy; one's lower teeth are always good.

On either side of him sit three men.

The room is long, narrow, and the heavy smoke creeps up and down, touching first one, then another, shuddering off. Seven bowls of soup stand at regular intervals upon the table. The imprint of foreign hostelries is upon the silver. On the walls, just behind the seven heads, are seven blue and white Dutch plates like halos, and above the seven plates the rising and placating star, a liquor license.

Tom Scarlett turns his face from side to side, brushing his shoulders as he does so with the ends of his long black sideburns. Like a bird whose wings have been plucked of their flight, this fall of hair seems to have been robbed of its support, clinging to the mouth, which was raised diagonally across fine yellow teeth. The head is magnificent and bald. Like a woman who is so beautiful that clothes instinctively fall from her, this head has risen above its hair in a moment of abandon known only to men who have drawn their feet out of their boots to walk awhile in the corridors of the mind.

His hands lie in front of him. They are long, white, convalescent hands, on which the dew of death is always apparent, the knuckles interrupting each pale space with a sudden symmetrical line of bone. These hands lie between the anchovies and the salt, and as he turns first to the right and then to the left, they move imperceptibly, as though reins were attached to them from the head.

And as Tom Scarlett snarls, Tash laughs.

Spave torments a pickle that lies in front of him with a fork, squiring drops of green juice upon the bare boards. Some of the others talk of a person of bad repute. One calls loudly for a glass of rum, while the sixth breaks, one after another, the backs of toothpicks, littering them over the floor.

They have been jesting among themselves because Tom Scarlett has been lonely again. They tell him that he has too many interests, and he answers: "Should one pass you over with nose keen for the most fragrant portion of your souls, where the flowers of your persistency have left their perfume, that nose would stop between your first and second knuckle, for on your smoke you have concentrated, as I on my flame."

They look at one another, and move among themselves, and finally are swept away in a great gale of laughter, whereat Tom Scarlett snarls and lets his face fall back into its habitual calmness.

The clock in the street strikes three. In the tolling of the bell the six hear the voice of their trade. For Tom Scarlett alone does it strike off another morning in man's short life.

For Spave it means that his counter is waiting his cheating barter; for Glaub, that the little pigs in his rotisserie lie feet upward in anticipation of the spit that shall be a staff on which to climb to the eminence of man's stomach; while for Shrive the ink is drying in his bottles used so illy to amuse men; and for Tash that the lumber in his yard is growing gray in the rain.

Freece seems to see his oils drying upon his canvas; while, last of all, it recalls to Umbas' mind the fact that there are three pretty little corpses waiting to be sent to heaven with becoming smiles upon their lips and a yard or two of lace bought at a great reduction for a dealer on Second Avenue, because slightly damaged, when his wife called him a fool and his hand shook.

To hurry matters, the six crane their necks in the direction of the kitchen, where Lizette is making sauce for the spaghetti. They cannot see, however, because Madame is sitting at her table drinking wine and snarling at her dog, and from time to time reaching down to rub forefinger and thumb in its hair, as though its fleas were her torment also. Tom Scarlett has often wondered how she kept her diners, so morose she is and so bitter. Her eyebrows twitch over her eyes like long, black whips goading her eyeballs on to hate and menace.

Spave balances an almond on his polished finger nail and sends it up, up, spinning into the air, where it turns, striking Madame's glass, dashing a blot of red upon the tablecloth. Madame opens her mouth, the eyebrows raise themselves as if to strike.

Spave leans forward, extending a stick of celery. "For your little teeth," he says, and Madame's jaws snap to like a grate.

But Tom Scarlett is annoyed, and because he is annoyed he realizes that he is different. Madame's eyes have become gamin; they search the men, darting here and there. One would say that they concealed a tongue, hid a mouth, cloaked a fist. Madame is always one course ahead of her diners. She seems to derive a great deal of pleasure from the fact. She is especially pleased if she can have one dish that they will not get at all.

The dog, like his mistress, is bad tempered in a tricky way, standing with one paw upon a bone—one morsel ahead of the yellow cur sniffing by the lintel. Sometimes this dog smiles, the saliva running in a silver rim around his lips, dropping tearwise slowly.

Tom Scarlett and the dog have something in common; both reproduce the atmosphere under which they serve—the one his mistress and the other his time.

Who is this Tom Scarlett?

His friends have ceased to idolize him because they have caught him picking his teeth. Thus many deities take the toboggan. They no longer marvel at him because he has given them to eat of the fruit of his soul—and because it was tropical and strange and they could not eat it, they said it was not eatable. Tom Scarlett snarls and offers them cigars, which they are more than glad to get.

"You are like a steak," they tell him; "good only when digested."

Tash beats upon his vest and howls.

"How you will be appreciated when his stomach has appropriated you."

Tom Scarlett answers quietly: "Still, I shall be the dish."

"But we the approval. A great man should keep several stomachs as he keeps a wine chest."

Tears bulge out Tom Scarlett's eyelids, but he answers gently: "I stand alone among men."

"So the flower thinks."

"Well?"

"There are always dead flowers to nourish the living, as there are always dead minds to support the steps of greatness."

Tom Scarlett smiles, exposing his fine teeth.

"I have crawled around the rim of the world like a fly—I know what I know." He leaned forward, placing his finger on Tash. "If men," he said, ruminatively, "were forty feet taller, the screaming of those in death would sound like crickets chirruping in the grass in the evening. The greatest kiss would be but a little puckering, which, when interrupted, would give out a fleshy sigh." He tosses up his hands, laughing greatly down the hairs of his beard.

"You will die as others die."

He answers: "Yes, I shall die as others die—crying out. But here I shall differ. A great man gives birth to himself; for him the death rattle is the wail of birth."

Spave spits: "He will put his hand upon his stomach as one in mortal pain, but he will cry, 'My head! My head!' a last transaction in favor of the mind."

And so they grew merry tormenting him.

One day they came later than usual. Madame was not drinking; instead she kept passing her hand back and forth across her dog's spine. She scowled, it is true, giving the room more of its usual morose aspect, thereby maintaining its cheerful air—for only by maintaining established custom are we entirely content. Still she shook her head in a way that seemed to give her a good deal of sorrow.

And they shook themselves because it was raining outside, a peculiar dampness that suggests to mind the fact that all things must attach themselves to some ailment, even men, reminded them that the earth draws much back to herself in her rainstorms beside the growing river and the Autumn leaves. So they shuddered, and Madame, eating her Parmesan, shuddered also and spoke to them.

"He is walking again today."

She pointed upward, for Tom Scarlett lodged on the parlor floor.

"Ah, he will be down presently."

"I do not think so."

"You will see. One's stomach is always the gendarme of one's mind."

"But, listen."

Five of them try to, but Race, taking his coat off, knocks over a chair.

"Why in the name of the saints can't you be quiet?" they shouted, in the exasperated manner of men who, if thwarted in their silences, will at least not be thwarted in their uproars.

"It's well," said Madame, peeling an apple; "You could not hear him, anyway; one has to see him now."

"What is wrong?"

"He walks like a cat. Do you remember what a noise he used to make with his great feet, as though he wanted the furniture to know he approached." She clicked her tongue. "No more."

The six began at their soup. "He will come down, you will see." But when he failed to come at the appearance of the cheese and nuts they began to talk among themselves. They said, "What can this be?" And they said, "He has indeed altered: I no longer hear his great feet upon the boards. He had arrogant feet."

Old Tash chuckled.

"After all, in a monarchy or in a republic, it's us little men that count. We bear the children, then we sense that one among the lot is different. Is it not by our hand that its face is kept clean? Would it not be a dirty gamin running around the streets in tatters, holding up its hands to squint at the stars, but walking in prodigious puddles? Is it not our care that keeps the bib dry? Do we not hide our children's drool until they are old enough to hide it for themselves? And is it not by our hand that the child is fed, that he is brought up into manhood? Don't we print his books, don't we build his colleges, don't we sweep his streets, light his lamps, make his bed, and in the end is it not us who bury him, after building him that other house that he has peradventure to leave; and is it not we who write his biography? He may be the voice, but who are the ears? Eh? He may paint the pictures, but who are the eyes? He may be a rare flower, but who is the nose? He may have his head in the clouds, but who is the earth in which his feet are set?"

He gave vent to a loud, rich laugh, a laugh that wedged its way between much good eating to reach the ears of Madame. He leaned back, striking his vest, as a jockey strikes his horse, letting his breath escape him in that after-dinner sign indulged in by the rotund. "After all is said and done, Madame, is it not we, I ask you, who are the great importance of the earth?"

Madame raised her eyebrows.

"He walks like a cat. I do not like it."

"So softly?"

"So softly, little dusty footfalls, like a cat, a small, profound cat. Men walk that way when they have changed their minds."

She did not explain what she meant by the word profound.

"A little, dusty cat, with a gray nose from prowling in among what people call great facts. Why, will you tell me, have all great things to be dusted? Cathedrals and books and windmills?"

They lit their cigars.

Madame snapped: "Eh, eh, and bric-a-brac and the inside of all empty bowls, the floors of reservoirs have known the feet of the sparrows."

"You talk in riddles, Madame."

"I talk one language; you hear another."

"The dog wants a bone," they suggested, and assumed a calm mien.

They asked Glaub about his rotisserie, and why he did not eat of his own little pigs for a change.

He answered: "Can one eat his own child? The aroma from my little pigs is like a sigh going up to heaven; it almost placates me. No, no," he added, "I cannot eat my little pigs; others must do that for me. We leave our children's seasoning to the public; they are the ones who make them tender and profitable. So with my little bits of pork with features at one end and a little exclamation point of a tail at the other. It is a waste of nature's talents that she gives features to her meats, but there it is."

"There are some who say that the odor of a butcher's shop is delicious—and fattening."

Glaub shuddered.

Like buzzards these six had flapped about the life of Tom Scarlett in that little basement room where Madame served her persistent table d'hote, and as such carrion swoop down and take away the eyes of the dead that have been its light, they swooped down upon the brilliancies of Tom Scarlett, thinking, animal-like, that they had its radiance between their teeth. But it was only the empty husk of a thought because they could not understand.

For long months they had tormented him so. For many long months they had been content to eat food that was at best a hollow mockery, as such food is liable to be. But to Tom Scarlett there was some dire truth in what they said—for he realized that around and around such men as he circled such a six and such another six interminably; and Tom Scarlett knew that because of him they gathered undue radiance.

So today when Madame failed to drink her red wine, while she rubbed the back of her dog and scowled and would say nothing to them that was either hard and biting, or soft and unctuous, they were uncomfortable. Was it not raining outside, and had not dampness settled down to a tete-a-tete with the smoke that hung like a yellow rag before the nose of each as they picked their teeth?

Shrive took another sip of wine. "If this country," he was saying in a garrulous tone to Glaub at his left, "does not give more chance to its public men—eh, I admit," he added hastily at the opening of Glaub's mouth, "that there should be places for the men of importance, of course, like the President and the deans of colleges and strikebreakers, but there should be one or two exalted chairs for its minor poets and its journalists. We can't all have a great man on ice."

The other four heard the last part of the speech and burst out laughing.

"Here," they cried, "may the ice soon melt."

They started to rise, and Tash got as far as the bending of his knees. Madame turned around with a hand in the hair of her dog. Presently she drank again, looking at the door.

It had swung open and the face of Tom Scarlett peered between the jamb and the outer edge. Tash sat down.

There was something in the eye of Tom Scarlett today that they had not exactly expected to see. It was not the eye of an obscure celebrity like Tom.

He picked up an apple and bit into it.

"Ha!" he said, and once again, "Ha!" Then he burst into sudden laughter.

"Six great-little men," he shouted, abruptly, half shutting his eyes, and added sharply: "Carrion! The earth about the flower, the hand that holds the infant's mouth shut until it knows enough to be hypocritical about its saliva—" He jerked the apple away from his mouth. He bent forward until his long bathrobe touched the floor. Then his fine yellow teeth showed between his lips, held up a trifle crookedly, as a portiere upon a resplendent yet gloomy room.

"What are you now?" he demanded. "Sparrows—seaweed. No, no! Hold! Business men. Little, dirty, gravy-spilling bourgeoise! Hereafter you will find it difficult to swallow your bird seed."

He laughed again, sitting down among them. "Yah!" he cried, more gently. "A great man among men, that helped you to be something, but what will happen to your stature if I become a little man among little men?"

"Now what have you done?"

"I am growing my own flowers. I, too, am eating bird seed with the sparrows."

He put a handful of apple pits upon the table.
"I think I shall open a little piggery also. I shall twitter."
But tears bulged out his eyes.

The Jest of Jests

The name of the heroine of this story is the Madeleonette. Why, never seemed to matter any more than that the hero should have been called the Physician when he had never so much as seen a case of measles in his life.

The place of climax is Long Beach, but that you will not understand until you reach the very end, though I might as well warn you that it was there the Madeleonette and the Physician fell into each other's arms, much to the consternation of the "regulars" on the boardwalk.

However, there was a third party to this story, and his name was Josiah Illock, a small, good-for-nothing type of man, who looked as though he should have been laying drain pipes in a small suburban town rather than making love to the Madeleonette.

On the other hand, the Physician was tall and dark and even handsome. He wore a long, old-fashioned frock coat and gray tweed trousers, and had an habitual expression of forceful timidity. He kept his hands in his pockets much ot the time, with that backward thrust that made him seem to be encouraging his receding backbone.

Now both of the gentlemen loved the Madeleonette, or they said so, and love and advertisements must be believed. For Josiah, she was the lily of existence; for the Physician, she was the rock on which faith or a home is founded.

For herself the Madeleonette was only a fast aging woman, who had managed somehow to keep a certain amount of looks and some of youth's fine hair in spite of the ravages of time. She was a widow who had been left in rather comfortable circumstances. Her husband, who had been an antique collector, had supplied her with arm chairs, sofas and cabinets enough to have started a small museum, but I would hesitate to say that this fact had anything to do with the affections of the two gentlemen just mentioned.

When upon occasion these men met in her green and white parlor, they glared, for they hated each other heartily. The Physician did not waste time intriguing to do away with Josiah, but when Josiah was alone with the Madeleonette, he could speak of little else until he defeated his own plans and set the Madeleonette's heart over in the direction of the Physician.

Sometimes Josiah would say to her: "Some day you are going to wake up to the fact that the Physician is not as crazy about you as you think. All men begin by loving a woman for what she isn't and end by perceiving what she is. In the beginning they caress the skin with kisses, and in the end they puncture with the pistol."

"Great God!" the Madeleonette would cry. "Do you think so?"

And he would answer: "Always it's an instinct. Men shoot what they do not understand. That is, they track the lion instead of the fox. They bring to the bitter dust the highest flying hawk and to the pitfalls they at last drag the antelope."

"There are no pitfalls for the woman over forty," the Madeleonette would answer. "There's only one possibility for her, and that is she will end life on a sofa with hot bottles at head and feet."

"Look here," he said, leaning forward. "you know what I mean. Shooting is simple. A woman can get over that—if—" There was a long pause. "If," he finished, "he keeps right on loving her—but he won't. They never do."

"The Physician would die," she answered simply.

"Want to prove it?" Josiah questioned.

She looked at him a long time as a woman does who is taking chances.

"All right," she said at last. "It's worth it."

He talked on, sketching his plan, but she did not pay any attention until she heard him saying: 'I'll see to it that it's loaded with blanks, of course. All you have to do is to fall over and pretend dead. Stop breathing for a few seconds, but watch. If he really cares for you he will raise hell. If he doesn't, he'll merely leave the room with you and the revolver together to prove it suicide."

She laughed, "You're a fool, ain't you? As if any one, especially the Physician, were going to risk his neck, even if he does love me. What's he to shoot for?"

"A provocation."

"What provocation?"

"Jealousy," he answered, pretending to be absorbed in his cigar band.

"You're all crazy, you men," she said, dropping off into an acceptable silence.

In the meantime the Physician, who looked back upon a life of thirty-nine years of timid shudderings, catapulted out upon the veranda of his home and stood there breathing hard.

He was more than a timid man. Like a carpenter's foot rule, he was long and powerful in sections, but too apt to double up and cease his calculations. He adored bravery because he had none of it. It was his reason for his affection for the Madeleonette. He knew her for a brave woman. He had a rock, while she had only a lover.

"Yet," he reflected sanely, "one should test the Madeleonette. A woman without courage would be my ruin. I lack that quality so myself."

He watched a long dust gray line of children with a certain keen shrillness of breath that did more to eat up tobacco than forty mouths applied simultaneously.

Now while the Physician mused, the Madeleonette prepared for the death.

When a woman decides to lie down and play 'possum she always selects with fearful care her hosiery, her petticoats and her shoes.

The pumps that the Madeleonette picked out were chosen for the newness of soles, the petticoats for its lace and ribbons and the hosiery for its irreproachable unity.

In her daily life she had considered her hats, her gloves and her buckles. When she decided to lean back against destiny, she concentrated on her lingerie. She tied her laces tighter, powered her neck lower, put her fingers into rings, her neck into the willing slavery of a halter of pearls, and upon her face she put that fixed smile which advertises a perception of the angels.

There was a sharp ring of the far distant bell. She ran out into the kitchen to press the button—waited at the door for the ascending steps to turn into a man.

Josiah Illock came in, removed his hat and shuffled over to a chair. He sat there gasping.

"You like it?" she said, indicating her gown.

"It is beautiful," he assented. "What is it?"

"Chiffon. It falls nicely," she confided with a slight blush. "It falls nicely."

He grinned. "It's going to be the jest of jests, ain't it" he remarked guardedly. But there was a nervous twitching of his mind that betrayed itself in the muscles of his neck.

"Yes," she answered. "I've been practicing the fall, Josiah. I'm black and blue, but I have made it not only a fall, but a disaster. It has become an art."

"Um," he answered. "You love him pretty much, don't you."

"Quite a bit," she assented. "But I love art more." She tried to look natural.

"There must be some subtle, fine, masterful touch that will make him realize that not only has a candle been snuffed out, but that an arc light has given up its flame; not only that a soul has passed into the night, but that a professional has given her last performance on any stage; not only that a grave shall open for the Madeleonette, but that an abyss shall remain forever gaping."

Josiah Illock did not understand.

"What will you do?" he questioned.

"I shall die smoking a cigarette," she said and watched for the effect.

She knew that she was not going to die. Had not Josiah Illock assured her, and did not Josiah love her?

Once Juliet had done this thing.

"My God!" she said, and started toward the window. Sudden ideas always take us to the casement. The tears ran unmolested down her cheeks. "What if the Physician, swayed with remorse and with despair, should take the paper cutter or the curling irons and thrust them into his startled soul? What if he should lurch over to the window and fling himself to the pavement? What if he should tie a noose of handkerchiefs about his throat and spoil the gas fixture for the next tenant? What—"

The tears ceased. "What a fool I am," she thought as she smiled. "I should wake up directly."

She went back to her wardrobe to hunt for a becoming dress. She laid it out upon the bed and, taking the cologne bottle, doused a liberal quantity of its contents upon the chiffon exterior. Then she laid it to her nose to ascertain if it was scented within the bounds of delicacy.

Next she took her hair out of curl papers and combed it into a ravishing coiffure. Presently, with her feet in bronze slippers and her electric coffee pot beside her, she gave herself up to pleasant expectancy, while she set the social crackers straight.

His eyes narrowed. "I don't see anything professional in that, though perhaps you are right," he assented and took to making nervous movements. Then abruptly he caught her hand.

"Can't you transfer that affection to me? Really it would be safer—please, I love you."

She drew her hand back. "You're messing things up a good bit, Josiah. I can love no one but the Physician. It is more than a conviction; it is something that has been bitten into my heart as a rose bug bites a rose."

Josiah winced. "You wouldn't have to go through this business then," he commented.

She turned upon him. "Not go through this business? Why, this is dress rehearsal. I wouldn't stop if I were married to him. You're a fool, Josiah. I have left the pistol in the hall on the stand. You'd better put those blanks in," she added as he arose.

When he returned, she failed to notice that perspiration stood out upon his upper lip. She set the teapot on. The doorbell rang. They both started. She opened the door.

The Physician entered, hat in hand, and bowed over his fingers. Then they both stood up.

"Give me your hat," she said.

Then Joisah came in with his behavior calculated to enrage to the point of madness. First he put his arm about the waist of the Madeleonette and, second, he kissed her. Third he opened his mouth to say some cutting things, but a look in the Physician's face stopped him with his tongue raised. The The Physician was staring at the nodding pansies in their box at the window in a way that seemed to him little ease. Then with a long step he reached the door and, at the same instant, came the short contralto song of a revolver shot. The Madeleonette dropped over sideways, with her cigarette still in her fingers. As she hit the floor, an abrupt flare of smoke burst from between her lips and ascended slowly in a gravely widening ring.

There was silence which was in its turn broken by the shutting of a back door.

The Physician laughed. A short, sad and very disillusioned laugh, and tossed the weapon upon the couch. He did not lean over her to look into her face. He did not stoop to kiss her lips. He did not cross those still hands above her breast. Instead he reached for the handle of the door and was gone.

In an instant, like a cat the Madeleonette was on her feet. She whirled a chair against the jamb and, drawing her chin above the transom top, watched with blazing eyes the exit of the Physician.

She watched him pass down the carpeted stair and on the the lower landing. She caught a tune from "Chin-Chin" as he went. She said sadly: "Now I shall have that little fool Josiah running around calling me beloved."

She dropped to the floor as a plumb to the sod.

"Josiah!" she called.

There was no answer. She groped her way into the kitchen. It was empty.

She did not understand.

But one thing she did. It was growing in a widening pain. The Physician had been tested and found wanting.

He had not only tried to kill her and had, so far as he knew, but he had gone out as a man leaves a lavatory after washing his hands. She represented the suds after an experiment.

So that was the man he was. Just on outside appearances he had grown blindly jealous and flared up. Well, anyway, she knew him before it was too late. What was the matter with Josiah, though? Why had he bolted? She got up and went back into the parlor, where she wrote a note.

She even smiled now and finished the cigarette.

How frightened he would be when he found out that she was not dead after all. What would he not suffer in the way of humiliation and perception of his great inefficiency. How deliciously miserable he would be when he discovered he had lost her forever.

She went on to tell him of her trick to test him and added a bitter little jab such as women fashion. "I shall no longer darken the doors of this place, defiled as it is by its acquaintance with you. I am leaving—shall have left by the time this reaches you—for Long Beach. I shall need a little rest in which to recover from this wound."

She sent the note by messenger boy that it might reach its destination before the blood of self-accusation should recede from his cheeks.

Some five minutes later a small messenger boy appeared at the door. "No answer," he said, and departed with that casualness indulged in by Western Union children in the face of death and reunion.

The note was from the Physician.

"When you read this," it said, "I shall already be gone. I tested you and found you wanting. At the sound of a pistol shot you fainted. Oh, woman, that pistol was loaded with blanks! Ah, how shall I ever recover! You whom I loved—a coward! I shall always love you, but where I place that love there must I also have faith.

"Forever I leave this sad, disillusioned home. I go to Long Beach, there to recover a little of my former gaiety.

"P.S—By the way, as I went out I found a loaded revolver on the table. What is the meaning of this?"

The Madeleonette sat down sharply. "I'm the antelope all right," she said.

Thus it comes about that the second paragraph of this story is the last.

Prize Ticket 177

C lochette Brin felt pretty sure that no minister would the awakening gravel to her window, because Clochette had to admit that she was no longer young and alluring, that her voice had lost is color as a fading tulip loses its beauty, and her eyes were not so soft as they had once been, as the steel of strife had entered rather largely of late.

Therefore all that Clochette saw in her future was a good old age and a possible set of six rose-cluster, silver-plated after-dinner coffee spoons—if she could attain them.

Clochette Brin was a ticket seller. Into the hurry of five o'clock South Ferry workers and the breakfast-regretting uptowners she wedged her way in the morning and hoisted all of a passing fair form upon the high stool at the back of the wired opening of the ticket window. Perched there like a great god on a human scale, between the cracker box and the old roped-in chair, sagging and falling in like the knees of an ancient woman.

In the very beginning, when Clochette had been young, she knew that love and lottery went together, as do heaven and harp. Also she reckoned that no matter what number your lot was set on, premiums were not worth much anyhow.

Incidentally, Clochette was nearly right.

Now at the age of thirty she knew that life was altogether a lottery of a baser sort. Therfore, she passed out the change with a heroism that goes with a woman who has become a little overheavy.

Whistling a popular air between bites of a ham sandwich and trips to the stove to stir coffee with a tarnished spoon, Clochette spent her life.

Her only family tie was a hard and uncompromising knot, a crippled mother, who hooped out the under side of a rose strewn coverlet, a living trellis.

Some women, as they grow old, lose faith and avoirdupois and, sitting on hard lean cane, go down life's pages an exclamation point, to slip at last like a splinter into the River Styx. But not so Clochette, for, having lived in the shadow of many heavy dinners, she gloried in the fact that she would make some considerable splash when she went in over the side.

Clochette did not mind passing on with the fraternity of the Silent Cold, but she would continue to object until she had as many silver spoons to call her own as had a certain very small roomer on the floor below.

Du Berry was her name, this certain small roomer, and she was delicately pink and fresh, and had hair that curled above bewitching pale ears, and she smiled so that she maddened men. She painted porcelain or something, and spent most of her time hanging out of the window.

She knew nothing of the world that had made Clochette's eyes hard. She had a gentle, generous heart, and she would have given Clochette anything she wanted if Clochette had asked. As it was, Du Berry knew Clochette only as an animated roll of "I" tickets that got unreamed by six of an evening, and then came home to be fed.

Du Berry was young and clean and wholesome, and pretty without powder, but having merely a back sink knowledge of Clochette, which lasted only through the washing of two potatoes, she never proffered her friendship.

There had come to the street a young man. He might have been twenty-five—a lean, dark, handsome, black-haired youth with a dilatory lilt.

He had no parents, nor relations, little money and apparently no occupation, at least this is the set of conclusions that most of the street came to in regard to him. A man who has an occupation does not lie in bed until ten or eleven o'clock of a morning, and yet a man without one seldom comes in by seven at night to do Indian club and dumbbell practice.

This much Clochette and Du Berry knew of him; the shadows in his room knew more. They knew that he was making himself a personal proposition by adjusting a face strap under his chin just before getting into bed, and by pulling much bath towel across a perfect Grecian back while he waited for the water to boil. Also the shadows knew that the weight of such authors as George Sand, Meredith, Moore and Dumas were the ones responsible for the knife-like crease in the young gentleman's trousers.

Doik was his name. Slender-handed as a pickpocket and warm-hearted as an Irishman, Doik crept into the street that now sheltered Du Berry and Clochette, the ticketseller.

Of course, Du Berry fell in love at first sight, as you all expected, and she would have asked nothing better than to have ironed out the white shirts that flapped from his window.

Clochette loved him also, but Clochette was different. She wanted to cook herring for his breakfast and take the lovers out of his cup of tea.

It was Clochette who got acquainted first.

It came through Doik's determination to have some sort of social life. He desired friendship. He also aspired to a better knowledge of The Avenue and of fragile teacups and the well-waxed mustache. He had heard that on The Avenue love and life were ripe for the picking, and he had seen the bus framed in the cut running south of Twenty-third street.

In the meantime he talked to Clochette.

Clochette talked well because she had a great scorn for the rules of the seven-foot bookcase, and these things made her very human.

She knew that Doik was broke, that he was a gentleman, that he was extremely well built, that he might be called handsome, but beauty goes at naught in Baxter Street as a substitute for cash.

He was hoping silently to move uptown. It was while he hoped and waited that he heard from Clochette about the two yearly events in Baxter Street.

Event number one was the arrival of the man from the boggy parts of London, who did tricks on stilts. And event number two was the annual prize given by Loggie's moving picture house for unmarried women only.

"Ain't you never been there?" she asked, thrusting a hand back in the direction of Loggie's.

Doik shook his head.

"It's the darndest swell place," she went on. "They have regular prizes every Friday, and once a year, upon May 5, they have the lottery set aside for unmarried women only!"

She tossed her head a bit and smiled, liking to think that there was such preparation for the unattached women of the streets of the modern Babylon. It gave them a sort of dignity.

"The other prizes are about the same. Anyone can get in on them, but this isn't silver brushes and table scarfs, it's the regular thing."

"Um," assented Doik, "and what is it going to be this time?"

"You can't never tell," Clochette said, with averted eyes. "It's generally personal. Once they put up a joke on us. We women were all there, and we was all single, too, mind you, and all of us was in a flutter trying to make out of our numbers the winning one. The little painter girl, Du Berry, was there, too, when the award was given."

"And what was it?" Doik leaned closer.

"Wasn't nothing much," evaded Clochette.

"You ought to tell me, you know."

"Why?"

Doik reflected. Girls had been telling him things for a long while. He knew that he had a finely-developed capacity for absorbing. Also he knew that nothing is withheld from Adonis, therefore he smiled and showed a fine row of even teeth. "Aw, come on, be a sport and tell Doik!"

She blushed and stirred up the grounds in the coffee pot.

"One of 'em was a teething ring, 'tother was—"

"Yes?" he prompted.

"A smoking jacket."

She raised her eyes to get the full of his understanding and he laughed suddenly, without sound, his hands upon his knees; laughed and took his hat off and said he was confounded, and fully realized what it must have meant to the sisterhood of Baxter Street. "Who got the coat?"

"Mrs. Penell's daughter, Daisy."

"Who got the teething ring?"

"I did."

He said he was confounded again, and stood staring in the direction of Loggie's.

"What is it going to be this time?"

"I don't know," Clochette answered. "Nobody knows until the last film."

"Seems rather hard on the married women," he hazarded.

"They should worry," retorted Clochette, off guard. "Don't they get all there is in life without wanting all of the prizes? Why, it's almost an incentive to stay single, and the Lord knows," she added, "we do need an incentive."

"Yes," he said, "I suppose so—say!—" he halted, and suddenly darted off and down the stairs.

An hour later the boy was seen striding in the direction of Sam's lunch room, and three passengers in the street said they saw him bolting beef stew and a large wedge of apple pie, "and," they observed, "eating it as though he had almost forgotten how." Which he nearly had.

Clochette saw him again about two and asked him, from the tired depths of her, where he had been.

"You see," he said, "I had a dinner coming to me. So I went to it."

"I see," remarked Clochette, and added: "Say, when was you home last?"

"I haven't got any home."

"No home. Say, Doik—kid—you—ain't an orphan?"

He nodded.

"No relatives?"

"None. Last of my family, last of my name."

"No friends?"

"Only you."

"My Gawd, what are you going to do?"

"I'll stick it out," he said bravely.

"Look here," she said abruptly. "You can come up to see me any evening you like, and me and my mother will try to make up for relations lost."

"You're awfully good," he said, and a film of tears passed across his eyes and sent into twisted lines the walls of the cage wherein sat his only friend.

"You can come up tonight," she added, and turned away.

The little painter girl, sitting with her feet up on the sofa and a drawing board in her lap, sang softly in the coming glow of evening. The odor of second-hand clothes and the labor of warm multitudes came to her. There had been such an evening as this once in Babylon. And now the wondrous incense was Pete's dray of onions and the wondrous flowing garments were Mrs. O'Shay's as she sipped lemonade upon the roof of her tenement. The soft sounds of an old world were just the ordinary high-pitched tones of Mrs. Skindisky calling her kids home.

The red lights gleamed down by Loggie's—the heart's blood to a never dead desire. The postbox had grown into the dim proportions of tomorrow's possibilities, and the gold and

purple bottles in the apothecary's window took on a highlight
as Danny, the druggist, turned the gas on.

Presently Du Berry put down the board and leaned out the
window. The police station was waking into a flurry of lights,
and a uniform or two stood upon the steps. The sharp
shattered laughter of a girl reached Du Berry's ears, and she
slowly turned her head and was sorry and somewhat sad. And
then, returning to the lights of Loggie's, she smiled and passed
indifferently on to the interminable ranges of tenement upon
tenement stretching away into the unlimited reaches of the
evening sun, and she started and drew in her head.

There was a step upon the stairs.

No one came up after Clochette, and she had closed her
door a whole hour past. The step was a man's too, and it was
light and almost hopeful, yet hesitant.

Du Berry's heart swung in great sweeps as she leaned
weakly against the wall. Was it—could it be?

It paused, and then it went up and on, and she stood still
and grasped the knob in her hand, and then as the step died
out, she opened the door swiftly and leaned out. For one
second she saw the blue of Doik's trousers, and the next, the
blue had passed into Clochette's apartment.

But the thing that had stopped her heart was the look the
owner of them had shot at her.

Remembering this same evening, it gave Clochette much to
regret.

"No, thank you," said Doik, shaking the crumbs off his
knees. "I don't think I will have any more."

"Can't I read to you, ma'am, or do something to have made
this an evening for you as well as me?" He said it so simply,
and in such good faith, and he held his hands so tight, and

looked so kind and funny, that the woman beneath the counterpane suddenly found anguish in her dumbness, and regretted, with full eyes, the fact that her limbs had been taken into the ample palm of rheumatism.

"She can't understand you," Clochette said, but she turned around and stirred something in a pitcher.

The boy wandered aimlessly about, and said presently: "Can't she hear, don't you think?"

"Yes, she can hear," said Clochette.

Sitting beside her, he read to her, and Clochette, watching, wondered sometimes at the things that Baxter Street gets in its net.

She helped him on with his coat. "You're a good boy," she said, and something in her voice made him nod a little as he reached the door.

"You wouldn't be proud, or glad, to see me sell myself, would you?" he questioned, and not waiting for an answer, thanked her and told her he would come again, and shut the door.

Now Du Berry never stayed up this late, but she heard the door of Clochette's room open and she heard it shut, and swiftly coming out into the hall, because she wanted to see him, she found herself looking into his face without an excuse, so she took his hands, and they stood so for a minute. The life of the street died down, and the horses in the stable by Pete's sagged against their stalls and stamped at the length of a Baxter Street night. But this did not affect the lives of the boy who swung dumbbells and the girl who painted porcelain.

And then he blurted out: "Are you going, too?" and she answered "Yes," and he disappeared in the night, which held also the colored bottles in Danny's apothecary shop.

Was she going? Well, she certainly guessed she was. The very next day she proved it to the whole street by buying the ticket two hours before opening time. You see, Tommy Thrupp, who sold the tickets, knew the winning number (sometimes they do, you know), and he, being fond of a certain lady who painted china, slipped it to her and told her, in a whisper that 54 was the rope around the neck of six rose cluster, silver-plated after-dinner coffee spoons.

After supper, while she was rinsing out the teapot, Du Berry told Clochette about it, out by the back sink, and Clochette's eyes hardened. "Six silver after-dinner spoons?" she said, and pondered. She looked this little frail girl over, and in her heart of hearts she knew that Du Berry was capable of giving up her life for the asking. But Clochette hated the asking of favors. And yet six rose cluster, silver-plated after-dinner coffee spoons just needed to make up the set.

"Say!" She turned so suddenly that Du Berry jumped. "Be a sport, will you? Take a chance. Let's swap tickets, mine is number 177. Let's see what will happen."

"But the spoons?" cried Du Berry, and opened her eyes, and then understood, and offered it immediately, and would have kissed Clochette besides. Therefore they swapped, and Du Berry went back into her room and closed the door, and said over and over: "Poor, poor old thing, poor dear, poor dear. I'm so glad I had it to give her. Oh! I hope Tommy was right."

The boy who played the piano at Loggie's grabbed the last handful of ragtime and sprinkled it over the audience in a closing crash of Spring sentiment, threw his knuckles into the back of the hardwood piano's trademark, threw his pompadour out of his eyes, and whirled around on his stool, accomplishing the death of the electric light over the sheets of music as he did so.

All of the sisterhood of the single waited in the dark along with Du Berry, who had come in late, and Clochette Brin, who had come in early.

One, two, three, of the sickly little lights blinked out of the dark at the side wings of the stage. Three, four, five, six, and Tommy stepped into view, whirling his great bag of numbers, and dashed to the middle of the stage, where (he hardly gave the numbers time) he proclaimed the winning number of the silver spoons to be 54, and waited.

There was a rustle as the whole of the maiden portion of Baxter Street focused their eyes upon their cards, the long disappointed sigh, as in full sight, Clochette Brin, the ticket seller, stood up, and with heroic Babylonian voice, told the residents of the unclaimed set of Baxter Street, that the rose cluster, silver-plated after-dinner spoons were hers.

Tommy's eyes roved a moment, and knowing Du Berry, smiled as he passed the prize over.

There was a stretching of necks as the sisterhood took in fully the person of the woman who had carried off their hopes.

And then all eyes went back to Tommy, who held up his hand. There was an awful silence. "The other winning number is 177," he said, and added, as Du Berry, breathless, half started from her chair: "Somebody is forfeiting her right to compete next year with this one. Allow me to present number 177."

Into the dim glow of the six lights upon the stage stepped—Doik. A little pale, his head thrust back, his chest unsteady. A splendid man in a moment when hard luck had brought him to this pass, and slowly his head came down level and he looked into the eyes of his fate.

"My Gawd!" breathed Clochette Brin, "I sold you, Doik, for a set of silver-plated spoons," and her voice broke, but Doik did not hear.

"Dear, the Lord has been merciful," said Doik, as he took the painter girl into his arms. "I got a hundred for this—and—you."

There was silence after that until one of them said: "I can't go again next year and compete for the prizes offered to"—a small catch in her voice—"unmarried ladies only—now," and something stopped the speech right there.

"No," said Clochette's voice out of the dark. "I ain't going to bother you, only I thought? (her voice rambled off in a strained and pathetic way), "I thought this might come in handy next year, when—you can't compete," and she was gone.

They struck a match, and, standing close together in its blur, they saw a little red india rubber teething ring.

A Sprinkle of Comedy

He was a tall man—with long, pale hands that swayed from the wrists like heavy flowers on slender stems. His eyes were long, pointed and blue with a curious spray of blood-veins running through them as though the eyeballs themselves were small berries set in the center of a vine. He had a peculiar way of walking, half lounging, and though he never gave the impression of being in a hurry, he somehow managed to get about a little quicker than anyone of his three friends. His hips flattened out abruptly from the base of the slender legs, and the bulging pockets of the tweed suit were always half full of paper clippings. A cigar usually hung in the corner of his mouth and sent an occasional wreath of smoke above the head which had already begun to lose its hair. The impression was the same as that obtained from a picture of a high mountain on which a cloud had descended. When he spoke it was in a short, sharp manner punctuated with an occasional drawled "and," "the," or "if."

He had done many things in his life, about which he told no one. He liked to think that he was yet able to astonish those few friends whom he had never even interested. Time and time again when he might have told his history with considerable profit he had failed to do so. Why? Probably because it had, after all, been dreary, commonplace, uneventful.

This man's friends were of the type that in an instant descend from "friend" into a "gang."

Djuna Barnes

It takes circumstances alone to make them either friend, lover, enemy, thief, brawler, what-not. It may be a hand on the shoulder, a word whispered in the ear, a certain combination of apparently unimportant incidents.

The man, Roger, knew this very well. In spite of his hesitant gait, in spite of his quietness, and in spite of his occasional quick speech, he had as yet not let them become aware of the fact that he was their master. He would sit among them, rubbing his chin, smoking his cigar, coughing, and say never a word. Sometimes he would drink with them, laugh when they were not laughing, remain immobile when they roared. It was only at such times as these that they would pause suddenly, and looking at him, break off with a half laugh or a counterfeit cough. He understood very well why. He never said anything.

This man had a wife and son. He never spoke of them, excepting once or twice when he mentioned his boy with a touch of ill-concealed pride.

His wife was the type of woman who, though large and sullen, always appears at parties and balls with a delicately fronded feather fan, or who is seen passing out of tea rooms with a long rose between her teeth—a thing that has probably been done by every woman in the world.

She carried her passion for flowers into her own room and from there to the windowsills of every window in the apartment. Window boxes of green sheltered pansies and violets in season, which she watered so often that they died.

Her flowers were second only to her passion for her son. For her husband she had the kind of peculiar approval that a woman often displays in public, by giving him too much sugar in his tea, and in leaving him entirely without it when dining alone. But for her, Roger would perhaps have been one of the great men of history.

The boy was frail and somewhat like his father—only shorter and more energetic. He had long, yellow hair, a straight nose, a manly chin, a great deal of plain honesty, and a marked talent for the piano. Yet at times, he would make short remarks warranted to anger his mother, who would raise her heavy eyebrows, and cause his father to move uneasily.

He was beginning to grow handsome and knew it. His attempt at a mustache had gone very well, and he twirled it so continuously that his finger-practice in the scales had markedly fallen off in the right hand.

He would say such things as: "It's no use, you needn't talk about the progress of civilization. We're nothing but expert monkeys."

"Ah, my dear."

"Yes, I know it doesn't sound nice—they haven't any manners. But that's the only difference, you see. Manners have franchised women to some extent—Shaw, for instance, has liberated them through the indefatigable politeness of his heroines' husbands. And no man was king until he had acquired the art of bowing without difficulty. The difference between the bow of the bourgeois and the aristocrat is, in the one, the face muscles are lazy and permit the cheeks and lips to fall forward, giving the face a sullen, ill-arranged look— while in the other, the face remains intact, even though you swing him feet first from a gibbet."

"My dear, you are what the English call horrid."

He twirled his light mustache. "You know I told you so," he said.

Then the mother would sigh, fold her handkerchief into a

very small square, and say to Roger, "I'm sorry, but it seems to me that the lad is growing strange and of an odd material."

Roger answered always in a flat monotone: "If he were material he would be silk," and clicking his heels together, departed to drink with his three friends in abstract silence.

What was his great fear? It was simple.

He feared that his son would grow weary of the same round of existence—yet at the same time he knew that he was capable of nothing new unless fate pushed him into it. This is the fundamental reason for the silence on his past; even to his son he never betrayed a knowledge of having lived before the age of 29. He hoped that his silence on this interval in his existence would prove a source of romantic speculation on the part of his son, and thereby, keep him a little closer to the family.

He desired an honorable career for his son. Why, we shall see.

He had suggested to him often the renown connected with chemistry. His son only laughed. He suggested a course in mathematics. His son answered instantly, "Two and two make five." He left that subject and went off into a eulogistic account of the life of an anthropologist. His son retorted, "Men have four legs, but they have learned to call two of them hands." His father sighed.

"Then why don't you go in for civil engineering?"

"To make a bridge," the son answered, "you burden a man with the things he loathes until, with his back bent to the ground, he once more calls his hands feet."

Roger turned from him suddenly and, pressing his hat over his eyes, went out into the street.

Well, what was he going to do about it? What did his son

want to do? Idle?

"Eh, eh," he would mutter to himself, "I'll teach him."

But when parents mutter that they will teach, it is about then that they are going to learn something.

Then one day his son came home without his mustache. Roger went into his own room and closed the door. There he paced back and forth for hours, his hands behind him, a strange look in his face, at once very sad and happy. In fact, he looked like a man who has just had a cup of cold water dashed into his face at the time that he has been presented with a material increase in salary.

Roger was perplexed on the one hand, and on the other, profoundly quiet. Something seemed to have broken in him, yet when he came out from that room later, a hard line had set about his mouth and shone coldly in his eyes.

As he went out, he fingered a little slip of paper earnestly and in complete absorption. He had placed it with the others in his bulging pockets.

He pushed open the door leading into the room so much frequented by himself and his three friends.

Finally, they were all silent.

They were even more than uneasy. Then they were startled. What they had been awaiting had come; what they had been expecting was about to happen. They felt themselves to be upon that brink which is called adventure, and which would change them for life from casual and uninteresting figures into something historic and terrible.

They ordered a round of beer and sandwiches. Of these Roger did not partake.

"No," he said as if in answer to something they had said in chorus. "No, boys, we don't need anything here but a little care and a great deal of alacrity."

One of them asked what was up.

"This," he said slowly, putting his hand upon his hip and softly reaching the fingers down by means of stretching them out to their entire length from the palm. "This is the matter—I need your combined help—do you understand?"

They assented.

"I also need secrecy—get that?"

They nodded.

"Can I depend upon you—all?"

They nodded a second time.

"You see, it can't be accomplished without your help, or I would do it alone. The boy is strong and I'm no longer young."

He placed the paper out smoothly in front of the three and looked up at them alternately as they read.

The note ran, in his son's hand: "It's all right. Charlie will make a great get-away tonight if it doesn't rain—if it does, we'll wait for a fair night. Don't exactly like starting an adventure that is likely to alter my life, in the rain."

And a straggling scrawl at the bottom of this: "Three cheers for the ever-increasing brotherhood of the ring!"

The men sat back.

"Well?"

They answered that they did not exactly get it.

Roger carefully explained: "It's my son, you see. He's always been threatening to run away. To become a circus rider at first was his idea. That was when he was 15. Then he wanted to be a policeman. And later, just lately, he didn't do a thing but read the sporting columns—that means that Jess Willard has got him by the soul. The rest of it is plain enough. He's going to run away with that boy friend of his, Charlie, a prize-fighter himself in a small way. That is, if it doesn't rain—"

The three of them answered: "What have we got to do?"

Roger answered instantly: "Stop him, of course."

"How?"

He laughed, crumpling the note up in the first fist they had seen him make.

"Now, why do you ask me such a question as that? How should one prevent one's children from dropping from the tree unless one scares them?"

"Well, what are we to do? Details!"

Roger placed both arms on the table with his hands locked at their ends. "First you must all come to my house. Second, you must have patience, much patience, because I'll have to put you in the cellar."

"Eh, that's cold," said one.

"It's necessary," Roger answered. "Then, when I give the signal, you all rush out and grab the kid. Give him the scare of his life and hand him over to me. Of course," he added, "I could reason with him tonight. Tell him that I have found out. Show him the note—but—"

He paused, looking around: "But that would not deter him for long. That sort of thing only fires a boy's imagination."

They were a little disappointed: "That's nothing very dangerous nor very interesting."

Roger smote the table with his fist. "To me," he answered, "to me—that is sufficient. To me it is important. It means my lad's future."

He turned away. There were tears in his eyes.

"Have you told your wife?"

He shook his head. "No," he said. "I don't want to worry

93

her—besides it will be sufficient for him that I know."

"Wouldn't it be better to catch him a little this side of the wood he has to pass at the end of the park?"

"No, no; the point is to prevent him from being successful enough to get three feet from the house—I want to—to—what is it they say—to nip this in the bud—I know to what it leads.

"Our children," he said, apparently unheedful for a moment where he was, "come to us and are content to stay with us only so long as the legs refuse to support them; only until they can hold the spoon, the glass and the fork themselves and then—they—fly." He added: "The child was right. We are monkeys, or something—we do not change. As soon as we can, we go; if it is a bird, it flies; if it is a calf, it walks; and if it is a fruit, it falls."

They whispered among themselves. His anger had altered them; his request for help pleased them, but his philosophy only puzzled them, made them laugh, which is often the same, because herein they realized lay the difference between the hand that does the deed and the brain that directs it.

They sat thus till toward dusk—then going arm in arm into the street they said that it looked like a stormy night, as there were no stars. They promised to come to Roger's house after dinner, and being cautioned to enter by the back way and to descend at once to the cellar, they parted.

The night had grown dark by 9:30, when Roger, excusing himself to his wife, descended to the cellar. His son had not put in an appearance for dinner—not unusual in itself, but tonight it made Roger unhappy and thoughtful.

Presently three knocks on the pane of glass at the windows warned him that his friends were without.

He whispered them to descend. In so doing their feet

seemed already to have learned to murmur where they had always shuffled and made a great noise. They were armed with long sticks and presented such a terrifying aspect that even Roger was pleased.

"I don't think it will rain," he said, opening the little window an inch and thrusting his hand out to feel the temperature and moisture of the night.

They spoke softly, which was not necessary, but which seemed to them appropriate. When we are about to trip a man up, we usually do it in an undertone.

Said one:

"When do you think he will come out?"

Roger answered: "Any minute now."

Said a second: "Is there a door nearer the front?"

"Here," said Roger.

They waited in silence; a long time passed. Off and on Roger slipped his hand out of the window chink to make sure that it was not raining. Off and on, also, the three men arranged the contour of their faces that they might look frightful, indeed, when the attack began.

At eleven o'clock Roger was walking up and down impatiently.

"He's late," he said, "unless he's waiting until I come home." Here he laughed a little.

He went again to the window: "I thought I heard steps," he said. He thrust his hand out of the window again. A fine mist-like rain struck it softly, wetting his wrist. He drew it in suddenly with a grunt. His whole figure relaxed.

"It's raining," he said.

They looked at one another.

"Well!"

"Let us have a drink. I will present you to my wife." He laughed again. "And my son."

They tramped heavily upstairs. Roger pushed open the door of the sitting-room, let his friends in and called to his wife.

"Here!" she answered, and came in presently with a slow movement, her sullen eyes peering ahead of her.

Roger went to the window and closed it.

"Why do you leave it open?" he asked. "It's cold, my dear."

"I know," she answered, moving lazily across the room as he began introducing his friends. "How do you do? Yes, I left it open when I watered the pansies a minute ago. Sorry."

With a half cry, Roger sprang toward her. "When you what?" he demanded.

Very slowly he sat down. He put his hands to his face and began to laugh in a hard, catchy manner.

It was at this point that he changed from a silent man into a monologist.

Something had broken in him, and what had broken was his own repressed soul in the breaking away of his only son.

He made only one allusion to what had just passed before he launched out into a torrent of words about his youth.

"Gentlemen, you see by what a father and son are parted." He cleared his throat, and spreading both hands open in front of him, began:

"Well, in eighteen hundred and thirty-nine, I, having long desired to become a prizefighter, left my father's house one night by a back window. * * *"

He was a gentle, childish man now. His friends sat and stared in rather a frightened way at three sticks of wood which lay on the carpet at their feet.

"Una and Lena were like two fine horses"

The Earth

U na and Lena were like two fine horses, horses one sees in the early dawn eating slowly, swaying from side to side, horses that plough, never in a hurry, but always accomplishing something. They were Polish women who worked a farm day in and day out, saying little, thinking little, feeling little, with eyes devoid of everything save a crafty sparkle which now and then was quite noticeable in Una, the elder. Lena dreamed more, if one can call the silences of an animal dreams. For hours she would look off into the skyline, her hairless lids fixed, a strange metallic quality in the irises themselves. She had such pale eyebrows that they were scarcely visible, and this, coupled with her wide-eyed silences, gave her a half-mad expression. Her heavy peasant face was fringed by a bang of red hair like a woolen tablespread, a color at once strange and attractive, an obstinate color, a color that seemed to make Lena feel something alien and bad-tempered had settled over her forehead; for, from time to time, she would wrinkle up her heavy white skin and shake her head.

Una never showed her hair. A figured handkerchief always covered it, though it was pretty enough, of that sullen blonde type that one sees on the heads of children who run in the sun.

Originally the farm had been their father's. When he died he left it to them in a strange manner. He feared separation or quarrel in the family, and therefore had bequeathed every other foot to Una, beginning with the first foot at the fence, and every other foot to Lena, beginning with the second. So the two girls ploughed and furrowed and transplanted and garnered a rich harvest each year, neither disputing her inheritance. They worked silently side by side, uncomplaining. Neither do orchards complain when their branches flower and fruit and become heavy. Neither does the earth complain when wounded with the plough, healing up to give birth to flowers and to vegetables.

After long months of saving, they had built a house, into which they moved their furniture and an uncle, Karl, who had gone mad while gathering the hay.

They did not evince surprise nor show regret. Madness to us means reversion; to such people as Una and Lena it meant progression. Now their uncle had entered into a land beyond them, the land of fancy. For fifty years he had been as they were, silent, hard-working, unimaginative. Then all of a sudden, like a scholar passing his degree, he had gone up into another form, where he spoke of things that only people who have renounced the soil speak of—strange, fanciful, unimportant things, things to stand in awe of, because they discuss neither profits nor loss.

When Karl would strike suddenly into his moaning, they would listen awhile in the field as dogs listen to a familiar cry, and presently Lena would move off to rub him down in the same hard-palmed way she would press the long bag that held the grapes in preserving time.

Una had gone to school just long enough to learn to spell

her name with difficulty and to add. Lena had somehow escaped. She neither wrote her name nor figured; she was content that Una could do "the business." She did not see that with addition comes the knowledge that two and two make four and that four are better than two. That she would some day be the victim of knavery, treachery or deceit never entered her head. For her, it was quite settled that here they would live and here they would die. There was a family grave-yard on the land where two generations had been buried. And here Una supposed she, too, would rest when her wick no longer answered to the oil.

The land was hers and Una's. What they made of it was shared, what they lost was shared, and what they took to themselves out of it was shared also. When the pickle season went well and none of the horses died, she and her sister would drive into town to buy new boots and a ruffle for the Sabbath. And if everything shone upon them and all the crops brought good prices, they added a few bits of furniture to their small supply, or bought more silver to hide away in the chest that would go to the sister that married first.

Which of them would come in for this chest Lena never troubled about. She would sit for long hours after the field was cleared, saying nothing, looking away into the horizon, perhaps tossing a pebble down the hill, listening for its echo in the ravine.

She did not even speculate on the way Una looked upon matters. Una was her sister; that was sufficient. One's right arm is always accompanied by one's left. Lena had not learned that left arms sometimes steal while right arms are vibrating under the handshake of friendship.

Sometimes Uncle Karl would get away from Lena and, striding over bog and hedge, dash into a neighboring farm, and there make trouble for the owner. At such times, Lena would lead him home, in the same unperturbed manner in which she drove the cows. Once a man had brought him back.

This man was Swedish, pale-faced, with a certain keenness of glance that gave one a suspicion that he had an occasional thought that did not run on farming. He was broad of shoulder, standing some six feet three. He had come to see Una many times after this. Standing by the door of an evening, he would turn his head and shoulders from side to side, looking first at one sister and then at the other. He had those pale, well-shaped lips that give the impression that they must be comfortable to the wearer. From time to time, he wetted them with a quick plunge of his tongue.

He always wore brown overalls, baggy at the knee, and lighter in color where he leaned on his elbows. The sisters had learned the first day that he was "help" for the owner of the adjoining farm. They grunted their approval and asked him what wages he got. When he said a dollar and a half and board all through the Winter season, Una smiled upon him.

"Good pay," she said, and offered him a glass of mulled wine.

Lena said nothing. Hands on hips, she watched him, or looked up into the sky. Lena was still young and the night yet appealed to her. She liked the Swede too. He was compact and big and "well bred." By this she meant what is meant

when she said the same thing of a horse. He had quality—
which meant the same thing through her fingers. And he was
"all right" in the same way soil is all right for securing profits. In
other words, he was healthy and was making a living.

At first he had looked oftenest at Lena. Hers was the softer
face of two faces as hard as stone. About her chin was a
pointed excellence that might have meant that at times she
could look kindly, might at times attain sweetness in her slow
smile, a smile that drew lips reluctantly across very large fine
teeth. It was a smile that in time might make one think more of
these lips than of the teeth, instead of more of the teeth than
the lips, as was as yet the case.

In Una's chin lurked a devil. It turned in under the lower lip
secretively. Una's face was an unbroken block of calculation,
saving where, upon her upper lip, a little down of hair
fluttered.

Yet it gave one an uncanny feeling. It made one think of a
tassel on a hammer.

Una had marked this Swede for her own. She went to all
the trouble that was in her to give him the equivalent of the
society girl's most fetching glances. Una let him sit where she
stood, let him lounge when there was work to be done. Where
she would have set anyone else to peeling potatoes, to him
she offered wine or flat beer, black bread and sour cakes.

Lena did none of these things. She seemed to scorn him,
she pretended to be indifferent to him, she looked past him. If
she had been intelligent enough, she would have looked
through him.

For him her indifference was scorn, for him her quietness was disapproval, for him her unconcern was insult. Finally he left her alone, devoting his time to Una, calling for her often of a Sunday to take a long walk. Where to and why, it did not matter. To a festival at the church, to a pig killing, if one was going on a Sunday. Lena did not seem to mind. This was her purpose; she was by no means generous, she was by no means self-sacrificing. It simply never occurred to her that she could marry before her sister, who was the elder. In reality it was an impatience to be married that made her avoid Una's lover. As soon as Una was off her hands, then she, too, could think of marrying.

Una could not make her out at all. Sometimes she would call her to her and, standing arms akimbo, would stare at her for a good many minutes, so long that Lena would forget her and look off into the sky.

One day Una called Lena to her and asked her to make her mark at the bottom of a sheet of paper covered with hard cramped writing, Una's own.

"What is it?" asked Lena, taking the pen.

"Just saying that every other foot of this land is yours."

"That you know already, eh?" Lena announced, putting the pen down. Una gave it back to her.

"I know it, but I want you to write it—that every other foot of land is mine, beginning with the second foot from the fence."

Lena shrugged her shoulders. "What for?"

"The lawyers want it."

Lena signed her mark and laid down the pen. Presently she

began to shell peas. All of a sudden she shook her head.

"I thought," she said, "that second foot was mine—what?" She thrust the pan down toward her knees and sat staring at Una with wide, suspicious eyes.

"Yah," affirmed Una, who had just locked the paper up in a box.

Lena wrinkled her forehead, thereby bringing the red fringe a little nearer her eyes.

"But you made me sign it that it was you, hey?"

"Yah," Una assented, setting the water on to boil for tea.

"Why?" inquired Una.

"To make more land," Una replied, and grinned.

"More land?" queried Lena, putting the pan of peas upon the table and standing up. "What do you mean?"

"More land for me," Una answered complacently.

Lena could not understand and began to rub her hands. She picked up a pod and snapped it in her teeth.

"But I was satisfied," she said, "with the land as it was. I don't want more."

"I do," answered Una.

"Does it make me more?" Lena asked suspiciously, leaning a little forward.

"It makes you," Una answered, "nothing. Now you stay by me as helper—"

Then Lena understood. She stood stock still for a second. Suddenly she picked up the breadknife and, lurching forward, cried out: "You take my land from me—"

Una dodged, grasped the hand with the knife, brought it down, took it away placidly, pushed Lena off and repeated: "Now you work just the same, but for me—why you so angry?"

No tears came to Lena's help. And had they done so, they would have hissed against the flaming steel of her eyeballs. In a level tone thick with a terrible and sudden hate, she said: "You know what you have done—eh? Yes, you have taken away the fruit trees from me, you have taken away the place where I worked for years, you have robbed me of my crops, you have stolen the harvest—that is well—but you have taken away from me the grave, too. The place where I live you have robbed me of and the place where I go when I die. I would have worked for you perhaps—but," she struck her breast, "when I die I die for myself." Then she turned and left the house.

She went directly to the barn. Taking the two stallions out, she harnessed them to the carriage. With as little noise as possible she got them into the driveway. Then climbing in and securing the whip in one hand and the reins fast in the other, she cried aloud in a hoarse voice: "Ahya you little dog. Watch me ride!" Then as Una came running to the door, Lena shouted back, turning in the trap: "I take from you too." And flinging the whip across the horses, she disappeared in a whirl of dust.

Una stood there shading her eyes with her hand. She had never seen Lena angry, therefore she thought she had gone mad as her uncle before her. That she had played Lena a dirty trick, she fully realized, but that Lena should realize it also, she had not counted on.

She wondered when Lena would come back with the horses. She even prepared a meal for two.

Lena did not come back. Una waited up till dawn. She was more frightened about the horses than she was about her sister; the horses represented six hundred dollars, while Lena only represented a relative. In the morning, she scolded Karl for giving mad blood to the family. Then toward the second evening, she waited for the Swede.

The evening passed as the others. The Swedish working man did not come.

Una was distracted. She called in a neighbor and set the matter before him. He gave her some legal advice and left her bewildered.

Finally, at the end of that week, because neither horses nor Lena had appeared, and also because of the strange absence of the man who had been making love to her for some weeks, Una reported the matter to the local police. And ten days later they located the horses. The man driving them said that they had been sold to him by a young Polish woman who passed through his farm with a tall Swedish man late at night. She said that she had tried to sell them that day at a fair and had been unable to part with them, and finally let them go to him at a low price. He added that he had paid three hundred dollars for them. Una bought them back at the figure, from hard earned savings, both of her own and Lena's

Then she waited. A sour hatred grew up within her and she moved about from acre to acre with her hired help like some great thing made of wood.

But she changed in her heart as the months passed. At times she almost regretted what she had done. After all, Lena had been quiet and hard working and her kin. It had been Lena, too, who had best quieted Karl. Without her he stormed and stamped about the house, and of late had begun to accuse her of having killed her sister.

Then one day Lena appeared carrying something on her arms, swaying it from side to side while the Swede hitched a fine mare to the barn door. Up the walk came Lena, singing, and behind her came her man.

Una stood still, impassible, quiet. As Lena reached her, she uncovered the bundle and held the baby up to her.

"Kiss it," she said. Without a word, Una bent at the waist and kissed it.

"Thank you," Lena said as she replaced the shawl. "Now you have left your mark. Now you have signed." She smiled.

The Swedish fellow was a little browned from the sun. He took his cap off, and stood there grinning awkwardly.

Lena pushed in at the door and sat down.

Una followed her. Behind Una came the father.

Karl was heard singing and stamping overhead. "Give her some molasses water and little cakes," he shouted, putting his head down through the trap door, and burst out laughing.

Una brought three glasses of wine. Leaning forward, she poked her finger into the baby's cheek to make it smile. "Tell me about it," she said.

Lena began: "Well, then I got him," she pointed to the awkward father. "And I put him in behind me and I took him to town and I marry him. And I explain to him. I say: 'She took my land from me, the flowers and the fruit and the green things. And she took the grave from me where I should lie—'"

* * * * *

And in the end they looked like fine horses, but one of them was a bit spirited.

The Head of Babylon

I t had been raining since Thursday. Furrows of muddy water ran across the stretches of road where the tufted grass had given out. The long ridge of moss and flowers that stretched itself like a snake through the town shook a little in the heavy gusts of rain. The cart with its flat cared tandem labored slowly up and into the misty valley beyond, always avoiding the band of flowers which separated one ox from the other. The whiffletrees shook, jangling their iron hooks, and the cooing of the crated doves came down the wind.

Some laborers from the adjoining town plodded past, their picks and shovels across their shoulders. Their tan jumpers dripped a mixture of rain and sweat. Some of them smoked pipes upside-down. They slouched by the general store with its dripping awning, and away into the gloomy fields beyond.

Behind a grove of elms surrounded by a small court and a row of fir trees, stood the house of Pontos—a heavily landed farmer of the city. Besides his cattle, amounting to several hundred head, he had some fifty fine horses, suitable both for ploughing and long team work. Pontos was a Pole, a tall, florid man, who always wore a black skull cap and long pale jacket. He had a small amount of knowledge connected with the problem presented to him each year by his land. His great ox eyes shone with a lazy good health. He stuck his thumbs beneath his girdle during the day while contemplating his crops, but of an evening he stuck them beneath his belt for pleasure as he looked over the heads gathered at his table.

His stomach and his house were both of the feudal type. A Roman would not have scoffed at the immense table running from one end of the room to he other. Nor would the epicure find it in his heart to sneer at his hung delightful hams with their sweet smoky taste and a tenderness that caused them to slip away beneath approving teeth.

Pontos had a great many children. He always alluded to them as one more finger than his hands. He would hold up his short fingers as he said this, counting along them, tapping them at the base of their hard topaz callouses, instead of on the tips—somehow he connected them in this way with his labor.

"There is Tina," he would say, going from the thumb to the first finger on, naming them until he reached the alternating thumb, and here he would finish, "And then there's Theeg."

His eleven children had grown up as healthily as his corn. They were all tall blond creatures with short upper lips and large ox-like eyes. Theeg alone resembled her mother. Her eyes were long and black and strange—lashes of silver covered them with a frosting of ice. Her nose was powerful where it flared into appreciative nostrils. Her mouth was small and well shaped. The upper lip was heavy and lay upon the lower languidly. Her cheek bones were high but not so broad as her father's, and her chin deserted the family entirely. It was small and pointed and soft and usually sought her shoulder.

The mother of these children had grown old suddenly, but with that age which takes a long time to become old. She had been a thin woman, but was now stout and small and wrinkled, with a color about her like the color of the earth.

Only her eyes had the same heavy silver lashes as her daughter's, and her mouth, too, had signs of having been at one time what Theeg's was now.

They were all good eaters and they were all fond of company. When Pontos kept open house it was for his family, his friends and his laborers. He saw no distinction in having risen to landowner. Somehow he connected it, in his mind, with his and his wife's and his children's hard, unending, untiring labor. He was much too dull of mind to be sharp of pride. He thanked God for his success and was glad when his friends and his "help" came to thank God with him. He needed help thanking God as he needed help in the harvest season. He figured that the more men there were, the heavier the harvest, and he let his landlust and crop law drift over into his belief in divinity. The more people giving praise, the more blessings.

On this particular night, his daughter was to be married to Slavin, a landowner in the neighboring village. Torches of wax had been set about the room. The youngest child crawled on its stomach, dabbling its fingers in the hot wax and smiling as it slowly hardened, covering its little hand with a white veil. At either end of the long room, two huge fireplaces were piled high with resin knots, while garlands of ground pine were stretched from rafter to rafter.

The table sagged in the middle like a loaded horse. Great white stalks of celery shot up from polished tumblers, and three yellow bowls of mush steamed on either side of a flank of venison. The musicians straggled in and took their places at the end of the room, tuning up their fiddles. One of them was an old Negro, who played through the Summer season in the small towns in return for food and beer. Now he was clapping his hands and smiling and cracking jokes and thumping with his feet. While his friend, after the manner of white people, tuned up his instrument, this negro tuned up his body, swaying this way and that, humming in the back of his throat and shaking his shoulders.

Pontos paid no heed to them, any more than he would have paid heed to the buzzing of flies over his pasties had he been a cook. Both stood for the same thing, appreciation of and participation in an excellent affair.

His wife sat in the old armchair at the foot of the table. For the occasion she had returned to the garments of her youth, a Polish dress of red and blue that had been worn in her seventeenth year. It had been altered now and made large around the waist. A handsome apron of yellow cloth with red and blue stitching lay across her knees, and for extra decoration she had removed her earrings.

The laborers who had been pushing their way through the rain in the twilight came in at the door now, shaking the mud from their heels and flinging their coats into a corner by the fire. One of them remarked that it looked like snow. Someone answered that it was likely; he had even known it to snow in June. Pontos did not desert his place by the lintel. Slavin had now shown up, and Pontos strained his ears trying to catch the sound of horses along the road that led away into the outlying village. The croaking of the frogs had ceased earlier in the evening, as if the rain had gotten into their throats. Across the stretch of cement yard, Pontos could see a bat hanging in a heavily branched tree, and beyond this the clouds seemed to be dispersing. Pontos rested one hand high up on the door jamb and laid his head against it, his large booted foot thrust back. His wife had begun to talk to some of the laborers, and a decanter of wine had already been unstopped.

Pontos looked upon his children much as he looked upon ungrown or unplanted stock. He hoped they would grow up well and marry well, as he trusted the seasons would treat his crops kindly. Theeg was his favorite; he could not quite make her out. She lay in bed all day like a child, yet he could not make up his mind or exact of his failing courage a caress that he would have been pleased to bestow upon her. He would have liked to stroke her beneath the chin. While still a child she had lost the entire use of her limbs, only moving her head and intelligent cold eyes; still, something in these eyes forbade that caress that always sprung to the tips of his fingers whenever he saw her turn her head in toward her shoulder.

Somehow he did not regret her unlikeness to her brothers and her sisters; if she had been corn he would have rooted her up, not being interested in natural phenomena and plant diseases; but with her it was only strange and different, and he did not resent her in the least. Somehow he liked and trusted her. That he trusted her, he never stopped to think about. Still, it was significant, as though he said, "I expect you to make the specimen one of the best."

A great dais was built for her at the head of the room between two long candles; a mat of flowers had been spread about this raised platform with its catafalque-like couch, and on the foot of the bed the little children of the neighborhood had littered small cakes and candles.

The priest had not yet arrived, though a great chair had been set for him near an open Bible. Pontos, leaning at the door, suddenly turned inward to survey the room, trying to see it as Slavin would see it, for he had heard the horses climbing the hill.

Slavin was a man who had started several local disputes in regard to agricultural improvements. He subscribed to several agricultural magazines, but seldom read them, feeling a sort of security in their mere presence. Sometimes he would take them to bed, but he never read more than three or four paragraphs before a feeling of great weariness would overcome him and he would fall asleep. Still, the other farmers considered him a dangerous unit, and found a great deal of satisfaction in the sight of his yearly crops, which were scarcely ever up to their own, owing to his many experiments.

He was a short dark-skinned man of about forty-five. He had fallen in love with Theeg at first sight; she seemed like something newer and stranger and more desirable because of her oddity. Tonight he was radiant but sad. He had stopped in at Leavitt's to get a drink before finishing the ascent of the hill, and Pontos caught the odor of it as Slavin's red lips moved beneath his bristling mustache.

He looked around eagerly for Theeg, and seeing the nest prepared for her, but without its bird, he went up to her mother, and dropping a heavy hand upon her shoulder, told her to cheer up.

She had been sitting in one of her contented and quiet moods, picking out the red threads of one of the embroidered flowers. She had such a profound expression of absolute and essential happiness that one would have found nothing astonishing in the fact had she mooed; but when Slavin told her to cheer up, two tears sprung instantly from her eyes and descended to her woolen waist, leaving brown spots as though she were of the earth.

The long table had already begun to fill before Slavin's arrival; now it was entirely surrounded by the friends and laborers not only of Pontos but of the bridegroom. Slavin would not sit down, but moved uneasily about the room. His stiff new shirt annoyed him, and he kept coughing a little. He had not dressed for the wedding excepting as such people dress. He had changed his boots and his collar and shirt, and had washed his face; and instead of speaking of the new mowing implements, so much in his mind lately, he spoke of the rain.

Finally they bore her in. Her four elder brothers were at the corners of a litter they had hastily constructed for the carrying. They placed her among the soft rugs of the couch upon the dais, where she looked like some splendid tranquil candied fruit with her heavy bands of dark hair and those strange silver lashes.

The great fires had been lit and the shavings caught, instantly shooting red and blue flames up the sides of the logs. Like gay colored lizards, they darted in and out, springing higher and higher at each renewed attempt.

Pontos was already experiencing that mingled feeling of loss and acquisition connected with the giving away in marriage of a favorite daughter. Theeg's mother, on the other hand, moved about hurriedly filling the tall glasses with fine old wine, and shouting, "You'll all drink now."

The priest had come in while the uproar was at its height and stood smacking his lips just behind Thalin, a younger brother who had his glass tilted over his nose.

Theeg had asked for a glass of wine, but in the excitement of drinking her health, she had been neglected. Now it was brought to her by one of her little brothers, who, reaching up to his full height and raising his arm above his head, could just touch it to her lips.

As she lay there, Theeg smiled. Her white feet showed below the fringe of the rug—one slipper hung loose at the heel, slippers that never touched the floor excepting when they fell.

The little cakes the children had strewn over the couch lay unheeded, and one or two of the candy bells had rolled down between her ankles.

Off and on, as they passed, the laborers took these cakes up and biting into them passed some remark to their neighbor.

The musicians were beginning to play snatches from songs, and the men were looking furtively at the steaming pasties that the cook had just brought in.

The priest began the ceremony, and it became mingled with the remarks of the mother asking her daughter if she was comfortable, and Theeg's answer to this question, "Yes," was taken for the answer to "Will you take this man?"

The night had grown dark outside, and as they feasted, the heavy rain could be heard dripping on the roof with a sound as though many fearful and light-footed animals were pacing up and down.

And as they ate and drank and grew loud under the wine, Pontos turned from time to time to look at his daughter where she lay upon her rugs. There was something in his heart that had not been there. Was it because Theeg was better than they? Because she was different merely? So from time to time the back of Pontos' neck gathered two long whitish creases where he turned his head; and from time to time he looked at

Slavin wondering what Theeg would think of him later.

And once the merriment reached that point where drunkenness follows, Theeg's voice could be heard high above all, "The land is their land, and the house is their house, my father's and my father's people and their children. And the cows in the field are their cows, and the calves are their young, and the things that grow in the Spring shall be theirs in the Fall. And all that's born for them in the Summer in long furrows shall be cut and die for them in the harvest. But this other is mine."

Some of them listened now; only her mother droned on as she picked at the embroidery, "The milk has been very poor this season; the cows don't get enough rain—"

Slavin got up; one of Theeg's slippers had fallen to the floor. He passed his hand over her foot gently before returning the little boot to its position.

"What was that?" Theeg inquired, raising her chin from her shoulder—"Thy hand, Slavin, or the earth?"

He laughed at the question and patted her.

Presently the torches gutted and went out one by one. The musicians had fallen asleep on their chairs. The priest dozed, his hands crossed over his stomach.

The trampling of horses in the court brought tears to the mother's eyes suddenly. Theeg was going now.

They dressed Theeg carefully in a long cloak of fur, and kissing her one after the other, the children filed by, standing in line, the first one looking back with a sensation of being a great distance from her sister.

Pontos got angry for a moment, and knocked Slavin in

passing; but he turned around instantly and smiled at him.

He went up to his daughter and kissed her on both cheeks. "A good, good child," he whispered, and made way for the mother. She was short and round, and could barely reach; her little stout arms on the side of the couch made her look as though she were leaning on a fence to gossip; but she was saying: "You will find it difficult. You will have to invent a way of living."

They bore Theeg out, and placed her in the center of the great wagon, and tucked the ends of the skin around her body. She began to laugh.

Slavin climbed in beside her, still shaking the hand of her brother. The driver, standing forward, took up the reins and the whip. Theeg spoke.

"Eh?" her father inquired.

"The glass of wine," she said, and, recalling, "and the little cakes."

She had the cakes put beside her, and Slavin took the glass.

She turned her head upon her shoulder: "Yea, the land and the moving things thereon, and all the young year that has begun, are theirs. All the grass that has found renewal, all the flowers that bloom, all the old hopes and the old manner —but this, this is mine. This new man and this new day are mine, and mine this task to make this lonely head a wild, grand thing upon its helpless pedestal." She began laughing again, the strange silver lashes shaking; and as the horses sprang forward under the driver's whip, the glass of wine spilled, staining the white fur.

The great peasant father looked after her. His gentle ox

eyes had closed a little as though the tears standing beneath them hurt.

"She'll make a great thing of it," he said, and tramped in. But he stood at the door again listening to the wind in the trees and the faint sound of the rain, and at the horses galloping along the road and down into the valley beyond.

The little one had fallen asleep in the puddle of wax, and her mother struck her as she lifted her up.

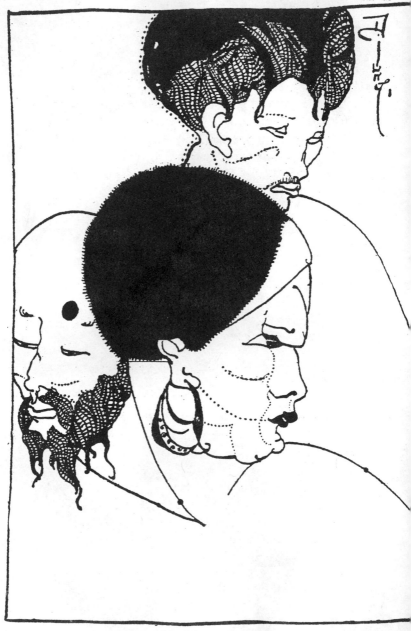

"And there was Zelka"

Smoke

There was Swart with his bushy head and Fenken with the half shut eyes and the grayish beard, and there also was Zelka with her big earrings and her closely bound inky hair, who had often been told that "she was very beautiful in a black way."

Ah, what a fine strong creature she had been, and what a fine strong creature her father, Fenken, had been before her, and what a specimen was her husband, Swart, with his gentle melancholy mouth and his strange strong eyes and his brown neck.

Fenken in his youth had loaded the cattle boats, and in his twilight of age he would sit in the round-backed chair by the open fireplace, his two trembling hands folded, and would talk of what he had been.

"A bony man I was, Zelka—my two knees as hard as a pavement, so that I clapped them with great discomfort to my own hands. Sometimes," he would add, with a twinkle in his old eyes, "I'd put you between them and my hand. It hurt less."

Zelka would turn her eyes on him slowly—they moved around into sight from under her eyebrows like the barrel of a well-kept gun; they were hard like metal and strong, and she was always conscious of them even in sleep. When she would close her eyes before saying her prayers, she would remark to Swart, "I draw the hood over the artillery." And Swart would smile, nodding his large head.

In the town these three were called the "Bullets"—when they

came down the street, little children sprang aside, not because they were afraid, but because they came so fast and brought with them something so healthy, something so potent, something unconquerable. Fenken could make his fingers snap against his palm like the crack of a cabby's whip just by shutting his hand abruptly, and he did this often, watching the gamin and smiling.

Swart, too, had his power, but there was a hint at something softer in him, something that made the lips kind when they were sternest, something that gave him a sad expression when he was thinking—something that had drawn Zelka to him in their first days of courting. "We Fenkens," she would say, "have iron in our veins—in yours I fear there's a little blood."

Zelka was cleanly. She washed her linen clean as though she were punishing the dirt. Had the linen been less durable there would have been holes in it from her knuckles in a six months. Everything Zelka cooked was tender—she had bruised it with her preparations.

And then Zelka's baby had come. A healthy, fat, little crying thing, with eyes like its father's and with its father's mouth. In vain did Zelka look for something about it that would give it away as one of the Fenken blood—it had a maddeningly tender way of stroking her face; its hair was finer than blown gold; and it squinted up its pale blue eyes when it fell over its nose. Sometimes Zelka would turn the baby around in bed, placing its little feet against her side, waiting for it to kick. And when it finally did, it was gently and without great strength and with much good humor. "Swart," Zelka would say, "your child in entirely human. I'm afraid all his veins run blood." And she would add to her father, "Sonny will never load the cattle ships."

When it was old enough to crawl, Zelka would get down on hands and knees and chase it about the little ash-littered room. The baby would crawl ahead of her, giggling and driving Zelka mad with a desire to stop and hug him. But when she roared behind him like a lion to make him hurry, the baby would roll over slowly, struggle into a sitting posture, and, putting his hand up, would sit staring at her as though he would like to study out something that made this difference between them.

When it was seven, it would escape from the house and wander down to the shore, and stand for hours watching the boats coming in, being loaded and unloaded. Once one of the men put the cattle belt about him and lowered him into the boat. He went down sadly, his little golden head drooping and his feet hanging down. When they brought him back on shore again and dusted him off they were puzzled at him—he had neither cried nor laughed. They said, "Didn't you like that?" And he had only answered by looking at them fixedly.

And when he grew up he was very tender to his mother, who had taken to shaking her head over him. Fenken had died the Summer of his grandchild's thirtieth year, so that after the funeral Swart had taken the round-backed chair for his own. And now he sat there with folded hands, but he never said what a strong lad he had been. Sometimes he would say, "Do you remember how Fenken used to snap his fingers together like a whip?" And Zelka would answer, "I do."

And finally, when her son married, Zelka was seen at the feast dressed in a short blue skirt, leaning upon Swart's arm, both of them still strong and handsome and capable of lifting the buckets of cider.

Zelka's son had chosen a strange woman for a wife: a little thin thing, with a tiny waistline and a narrow chest and a small, very lovely throat. She was the daughter of a ship owner and had a good deal of money in her name. When she married Zelka's son, she brought him some ten thousand a year. And so he stopped the shipping of cattle and went in for exports and imports of Oriental silks and perfumes.

When his mother and father died, he moved a little inland away from the sea and hired clerks to do his bidding. Still, he never forgot what his mother had said to him: "There must always be a little iron in the blood, sonny."

He reflected on this when he looked at Lief, his wife. He was a silent, taciturn man as he grew older, and Lief had grown afraid of him, because of his very kindness and his melancholy.

There was only one person to whom he was a bit stern, and this was his daughter, "Little Lief." Toward her he showed a strange hostility, a touch even of that fierceness that had been his mother's. Once she had rushed shrieking from his room because he had suddenly roared behind her as his mother had done behind him. When she was gone, he sat for a long time by his table, his hands stretched out in front of him, thinking.

He had succeeded well. He had multiplied his wife's money now into the many thousands—they had a house in the country and servants. They were spoken of in the town as a couple who had an existence that might be termed as "pretty soft"; and when the carriage drove by of a Sunday with baby Lief up front on her mother's lap and Lief's husband beside her in his gray cloth coat, they stood aside not be be trampled on by the swift legged, slender ankled "pacer" that Lief had bought that day when she had visited the "old home"—the beach that had known her and her husband when they were children. This horse was the very one that she had asked for when she saw how beautiful it was as they fastened the belt to it preparatory to lowering it over the side. It was then that she remembered how, when her husband had been a little boy, they had lowered him over into the boat with this same belting.

During the Winter that followed, which was a very hard one, Lief took cold and resorted to hot water bottles and thin tea. She became very fretful and annoyed at her husband's constant questionings as to her health. Even Little Lief was a nuisance because she was so noisy. She would steal into the room, and, crawling under her mother's bed, would begin to sing in a high, thin treble, pushing the ticking with her patent leather boots to see them crinkle. Then the mother would cry out, the nurse would run in and take her away, and Lief would spend a half hour in tears. Finally they would not allow Little Lief in the room, so she would steal by the door many times, walking noiselessly up and down the hall. But finally, her youth overcoming her, she would stretch her legs out into a straight goose step, and for this she was whipped because on the day that she had been caught, her mother had died.

And so the time passed and the years rolled on, taking their toll. It was now many Summers since that day that Zelka had walked into town with Swart—now many years since Fenken had snapped his fingers like a cabby's whip. Little Lief had never even heard that her grandmother had been called a "beautiful woman in a black sort of way," and she had only vaguely heard of the nickname that had once been given the family, the "Bullets." She came to know that great strength had once been in the family, to such an extent, indeed, that somehow a phrase was known to her, "Remember always to keep a little iron in the blood." And one night she had pricked her arm to see if there were iron in it, and she had cried because it hurt. And so she knew that there was none.

With her this phrase ended. She never repeated it because of that night when she had made that discovery.

Her father had taken to solitude and the study of sociology. Sometimes he would turn her about by the shoulder and look at her, breathing in a thick way he had with him of late. And once he told her she was a good girl but foolish, and left her alone.

They had begun to lose money, and some of Little Lief's tapestries, given her by her mother, were sold. Her heart broke, but she opened the windows oftener because she needed some kind of beauty. She made the mistake of loving tapestries best and nature second best. Somehow she had gotten the two things mixed—of course, it was due to her bringing up. "If you are poor, you live out-of-doors; but if you are rich, you live in a lovely house." So to her the greatest of calamities had befallen the house. It was beginning to go away by those imperceptible means that at first leave a house looking unfamiliar and then bare.

Finally she could stand it no longer and she married a thin, wiry man with a long, thin nose and a nasty trick of rubbing it with a finger equally long and thin—a man with a fair income and very refined sisters.

This man, Misha, wanted to be a lawyer. He studied half the night and never seemed happy unless his head was in his palm. His sisters were like this also, only for another reason: they enjoyed weeping. If they could find nothing to cry about, they cried for the annoyance of this dearth of destitution and worry. They held daily councils for future domestic trouble—one the gesture of emotional and one of mental desire.

Sometimes Little Lief's father would come to the big iron gate and ask to see her. He would never come in—why? He never explained. So Little Lief and he would talk over the gate top, and sometimes he was gentle and sometimes he was not. When he was harsh to her, Little Lief wept, and when she wept, he would look at her steadily from under his eyebrows and say nothing. Sometimes he asked her to take a walk with him. This would set Little Lief into a terrible flutter; the corners of her mouth would twitch and her nostrils tremble. But she always went.

Misha worried little about his wife. He was a very selfish man, with that greatest capacity of a selfish nature, the ability to labor untiringly for some one thing that he wanted and that nature had placed beyond his reach. Some people called this quality excellent, pointing out what a great scholar Misha was, holding him up as an example in their own households, looking after him when he went hurriedly down the street with that show of nervous expectancy that a man always betrays when he knows within himself that he is deficient—a sort of peering in the face of life to see if it has discovered the flaw.

Little Lief felt that her father was trying to be something that was not natural to him. What was it? As she grew older, she tried to puzzle it out. Now it happened more often that she would catch him looking at her in a strange way, and once she asked him half playfully if he wished she had been a boy. And he had answered abruptly, "Yes, I do."

Little Lief would stand for hours at the casement and, leaning her head against the glass, try to solve this thing about her father.

And then she discovered it when he had said, "Yes, I do." He was trying to be strong—what was it that was in the family?—oh, yes—iron in the blood. He feared there was no longer any iron left. Well, perhaps there wasn't—was that the reason he looked at her like this? No, he was worried about himself. Why?—wasn't he satisfied with his own strength? He had been cruel enough very often. This shouldn't have worried him.

She asked him, and he answered, "Yes, but cruelty isn't strength." That was an admission. She was less afraid of him since that day when he had made that answer, but now she kept peering into his face as he had done into hers, and he seemed not to notice it. Well, he was getting to be a very old man.

Then one day her two sisters-in-law pounced upon her so that her golden head shook on its thin, delicate neck.

"Your father has come into the garden," cried one.

"Yes, yes," pursued the elder. "He's even sat himself upon the bench."

She hurried out to him. "What's the matter, father?" Her head was aching.

"Nothing." He did not look up.

She sat down beside him, stroking his hand, at first timidly, then with more courage.

"Have you looked at the garden?"

He nodded.

She burst into tears.

He took his hand away from her and began to laugh.

"What's the matter, child? A good dose of hog-killing would do you good."

"You have no right to speak to me in this way—take yourself

off!" she cried sharply, holding her side. And her father rocked with laughter.

She stretched her long, thin arms out, clenching her thin fingers together. The lace on her short sleeves trembled, her knuckles grew white.

"A good pig-killing," he repeated, watching her. And she grew sullen.

"Eh?" He pinched her flesh a little and dropped it. She was passive; she made no murmur. He got up, walked to the gate, opened it and went out, closing it after him. He turned back a step and waved to her. She did not answer for a moment, then she waved back slowly with one of her thin, white hands.

She would have liked to refuse to see him again, but she lacked courage. She would say to herself, "If I am unkind to him now, perhaps later I shall regret it." In this way she tried to excuse herself. The very next time he had sent word that he wished speech with her, she had come.

"Little fool!" he said, in a terrible rage, and walked off. She was quite sure that he was slowly losing his mind—a second childhood, she called, it, still trying to make things as pleasant as possible.

She had been ill a good deal that Spring, and in the Fall she had terrible headaches. In the Winter months she took to her bed, and early in May the doctor was summoned.

Misha talked to the physician in the drawing-room before he sent him up to his wife.

"You must be gentle with her. She is nervous and frail." The doctor laughed outright. Misha's sisters were weeping, of course, and perfectly happy.

"It will be such a splendid thing for her," they said, meaning the beef, iron and wine that they expected the doctor to prescribe.

Toward evening Little Lief closed her eyes.

Her child was still-born.

The physician came downstairs and entered the parlor where Misha's sisters stood together, still shedding tears.

He rubbed his hands.

"Send Misha upstairs."

"He has gone."

"Isn't it dreadful? I never could bear corpses, especially little ones."

"A baby isn't a corpse," answered the physician, smiling at his own impending humor. "It's an interrupted plan."

He felt that the baby, not having drawn a breath in this would, could not feel hurt at such a remark, because it had gathered no feminine pride and, also, as it had passed out quicker than the time it took to make the observation, it really could be called nothing more than the background for medical jocularity.

Misha came into the room with red eyes.

"Out like a puff of smoke," he said.

One of the sisters remarked: "Well, the Fenkens lived themselves thin."

The next Summer Misha married into a healthy Swedish family. His second wife had a broad face, with eyes set wide apart, and with broad, flat, healthy, yellow teeth. And she played the piano surprisingly well, though she looked a little heavy as she sat upon the piano stool.

The Coward

Varra Kolveed had led too long that life of unending sameness that has its end either in hysteria or melancholy. Twice a day the bodies of her little sisters were pushed and patted and shoved by her into and out of their shabby clothing. At six o'clock precisely the day found her laying the table for her sister's husband, her sister herself, and for those same smaller ones that had come into their care with the death of her mother. Every afternoon and every evening saw her shaking out the red tablespread also, and at nine o'clock exactly, Varra descended the first two steps leading into the streed and waited for Karl.

Varra had been engaged to Karl going on three years now, and the three years were threatening to stretch into a fourth for lack of money. Romance had died there on that second step above the pavement and had given away to habit.

Varra had never been called pretty. She had even been termed rather plain. She had never admitted this judgment to be correct. She even thought, quite frankly, that she was a little more than passable. She had lived so long among dull things that anything with a bit of color in it seemed to her beautiful, and Varra had the red round spots high up on her cheeks that one sees occasionally in Breton peasants, and Varra had very splendid curling hair, which she had never allowed to grow long since it had been cropped the year of the fever—and this hair stood up on her head in a red flaming wedge which seemed to Varra very good.

One thing only had Varra that put her above those with whom she came in contact: she had what was called a reputation.

Just when this reputation began no one could remember; even Varra had forgotten. The incident that must have led to it was a thing of the past. Sometimes Varra tried to remember what it was that had given her this reputation for courage, as she plaited her hair before she went to bed. Was it that day that she had climbed across the roof and down into the gutter and saved the new Spring robin when all the boys were timid? Or was it when she had used a knife to take out a splinter one evening as she sat on the steps? She remembered this knife, a long thin polished blade that seemed to demand bravery. And then the girl across the way had been watching, so Varra had cut herself quite a deep gash, dabbing the blood off with her handkerchief, but taking care to fold the scarlet spots out, so that they would be conspicuous all that evening when she rubbed her nose or wiped her forehead.

Anyway there the reputation was. It had become very precious to Varra because it was someone else's opinion and not her own. But gradually it became her own, and she could not always recollect whether people had said she was beautiful or courageous until she stopped to consider which of these two qualities she had given herself involuntarily.

As Varra grew up she became very proud of this reputation. She nursed it, and at the same time it kept her in a great deal of anxiety. She had to keep thinking up little things that would remind the neighbors that she was this year what she had been last—the courage that had picked her out for attention then was still one of her qualities. In the end she thought herself a little braver than she really was. Sincerely and honestly, she held to this opinion and would have raged had she been denied this little grain of personal elations.

For Varra there had been little youth, just a few hours in the sun, just a moment snatched from romanticism with some novel of the time, one short little moment of an appreciation that Spring had come and Spring would go, one lilac bloom that had meant something to her, one moment when, lying face down in the June grass, she had waited silently for her chance, had finally caught the one bird that she could remember as having had freedom, one acknowledgment that night was mysterious and frightful and something to lie under as one would lie under a guillotine waiting for the moment when the knife should descend, the knife that must inevitably be there high up in the dark against the ceiling, the something portentous that gave her this feeling of impending doom, this tightening of the feet, this thanksgiving for the heavy weave of the sheet sensed against her nose and mouth and her closed lids.

And then Varra had gone past it, without memory when it stopped and without regrets for its ending because it had no definite boundary. And she only felt a sense that within her somewhere was an island surrounded by what she now was, that was, that had been her childhood.

Many times in the years that went to the making of Varra, she had silently regretted this name she bore for bravery. When a spider was seen about the place, it was she now who had to catch and kill it. The rest of the family had grown frankly timid as Varra had grown, to all appearances, more bold. When the frying pan handle was red hot, it was Varra who came up and took it off the stove in her bare hands, smiling. It was Varra also who had to part the pair of bull pups that had flown at one another's throats. It was she who put the ropes about their necks and she it was who finally parted them.

Once or twice in the beginning she had said timidly, "I am not so brave, you know," and they had all answered, "See, true courage. She is a brave child, yes, a modest one."

And then she had become engaged, and Karl flattered her and told her that he loved her for her bravery more than anything else. Karl's chum, Monk, had also flattered Varra. Indeed, toward the end of this third year of engagement, Varra had become so accustomed to this title that she no longer lay awake trying to remember where it had its begining.

She read fairy tales where damsels with wands ruled over a world of the timid. She was always finding herself in love with the hero and the heroine of some novel. She came out of them into her own life with a little gasp of sorrow, and she went back into them again with a sigh of content.

Yet Varra had still a certain kind of acuteness. There were things that she liked and there were things that she did not like at all. The only trouble was that she failed to keep her sense of values separate. She had been called brave, so now she thought it was brave to like people that her instinct bade her to distrust. Monk was a man that instinctively bred dislike. His ill-shaped head give her physical pain, and the wide low set ears,

"She had read of a world ruled by fairies"

set on at an angle seen commonly in monkeys, made her feel a repulsion for looking at him at all, and his jaunty, quick slang with its touch of false bravado made her unhappy because she sensed in this same bravado her own bravery; only in him there was something vulgar. The difference lay in this: he was trying to produce an illusion and Varra was trying not to disillusion.

And then had come that terrible hour when a little crowd collected about their door, overflowing into their parlor, talking all at once.

Karl and Monk had been arrested. Leaning with her forehead against the door, Varra tried to make out what they were saying. She put her hands to her throat and found it was not the spot that troubled her. Her hands slipped to her heart, and this was also lacking in appropriateness. She began untying her apron, and this was the gesture that seemed at last to be the right one. What was she doing? What were they saying? Robbery? Where? She pushed forward, still pulling at the knot in her apron.

"What is this?" she cried in a sharp voice.

"Karl and Monk have been arrested."

"What for?"

"They were under suspicion for some time—petty robberies, they said. —jewelry—and then last night quite a haul from the Barnaby place."

She wasn't listening any more. Jewelry? Karl? She brought her two hands around with the apron in them, feeling for the little cheap ring on her third finger. Tears slowly rose to the borders of her pale eyes. Then she heard her sister saying,

"You must be brave, dear."

Varra turned away and went upstairs.

She lay face up on the bed. This was another concession made to her reputation. She wanted to bury her eyes in the pillow, but she mustn't. What must she do? Get up, walk about? Yes, that was it—get up and walk about. Why? Where?

She went to the table and picked up a brooch Karl had given her. Stolen, too, eh? She rummaged through her bureau; a necklace of beads and a broad bracelet were all the things that she could remember as having come from Karl in their three years of courtship. She put these all together. She never stopped to question herself about her feeling in reaction to this change. She did not deny it to herself because in doing this she thought she would be a coward; and now she must show what she was really made of, if, indeed, she were a brave woman after all, or only a sham.

Toward eight o'clock, her sister knocked at her door.

"He is to be tried tomorrow," she whispered along the crack, and stole away again.

Suddenly Varra's courage gave out in one terrible storm of weeping, and she turned over on her bed heavily, pressing the bedding up around her as if she wanted to bury herself, to dig herself into oblivion. This reputation of hers had been built of the things the house was built of, the daily household sayings. It was in the atmosphere; it was a household quality, a something that had been given life to by all these things that surrounded her, and she abruptly realized that it was with the household that she was trying to bury herself. She sat up, throwing the blankets away with a quick, frightened gesture. She felt dizzy and tried to weep again and could not. She stood up before her little cracked mirror. Was she really ugly? The color had left her cheeks, but it was in her lips.

She knew now what it was that had really brought on this great fit of weeping—it was because she knew what she had before her and what she must do for Karl. What was it they had said? Oh yes, of course, she was courageous; she must begin now. Tomorrow, her little sister had said. She would have to find out where the court was.

The mid-day session was in full swing. Petty lawyers in frock coats promenaded the wide corridors like dogs on the track of game. Misery, despair, justice, injustice—all these things were their meal. They circled about this hall, their fat, small hands hidden in the tails of these sleek, shiny coats, and their bright, alert eyes darting here and there. One of these lawyers had been following a woman with his eyes for the last ten seconds as the woman stood in the shadow of the winding staircase, her hands clasped in front of her, holding a faded yellow box. She stood very still, seemed to impart something like importance to a case. Only after he had finished his pleading and retired behind the railings did the case again drop into its poverty and ugly despair once more.

He approached Varra now, his oiled black hair shining as he stepped across the bar of light falling in at the wide entrance.

"Are you represented?" he spoke softly, pleasantly, and he dropped his hands to his side, his coat tails swinging. He was very proud of this coat; it had been nicknamed the "Case coat," or the "Coat of appeals."

Varra turned toward him slowly and looked at him a

minute. Then she said, "What?" fearing that perhaps this man had something to do with the whole system of judicial ruling.

He repeated his question, adding that she really should have a lawyer. She shook her head and moved off. What she had to do must be done alone; therein lay the impetus. She did not need help to be courageous. She could save Karl alone. She could tell the lie that would set him free. She was strong enough to go straight up to the judge and pronounce the words that would throw suspicion on to herself. And besides, she had the necklace, the ring, the brooch and the bracelet, all together in this little yellow box. If they did not believe her, they would believe their eyes. How would she come by this plunder unless she herself had stolen it?

She moved toward the doors. She could see the benches filled with sleepy looking people. She felt herself rudely pushed aside by a German woman who was speaking in a shrill voice to the court attendant who would not let her pass. Varra felt very lonely. After all, what was the use; no one was here to help her; no one was here to know what she was doing. She should have told them at home. No, Karl would be the only one to know.

A feeling of tenderness swept over her for Karl. After, she loved him; and her own impending sacrifice made him seem newborn in all the splendor of the deed. She looked up into the face of the court attendant and smiled. "May I sit down and watch awhile?" she asked cunningly, hoping that he would be pleased with her and treat her as some one with a really superior nature, so it would give her confidence in herself.

He did like her frank smile, and the red-rimmed eyes looking up into his, coquettishly, made him stand aside for her, and made him watch her as she moved to a seat.

She leaned forward a little, looking straight ahead of her. There was the raised platform with the judicial desk. There were the clerks, the court stenographer, the petty lawyers, the police—the relatives weeping, the dry-eyed curiosity seekers. The man in black sitting with slightly bowed head behind the desk must be the judge. She looked around, but could not see either Karl or Monk. Some dreary prisoners were sitting back to her on a bench within the railing, and a reporter stood beside the clerks' desk, pad in hand. Why were all these people sitting here? What did they want to see? What they themselves had escaped, what they themselves would have some day to go through, perhaps?

The dirty black curtains, with their heavy tassels at the windows, took her attention. They were like the smaller curtains at the windows of a hearse, only the tassels were too terrible and too heavy. They seemed like judges that had grown sulky beneath their wigs of dust, like something that would finally fall into the cup of life and lie there, black and horrible and menacing, spoiling it at the lips, as mother spoils the beauty of wine, the malignity of vinegar.

Varra looked at the judge. She wondered why people neglect to make friends with judges, as it would help so if they were on a calling basis. If this judge had said to her once, "Please pass the tea, Miss Kolveed," she would now be able to go right up to him and whisper into his ear to be kind to Karl, and all would be over. But she had neglected to do this, and so it was going to make a difference.

Some mean case of some sort had just come up. Two men, one an officer and the other a Pole, stood before this bar of justice, holding up a strip of lace. She could not hear a word that was said, and she was glad. It would not spoil this great thing she had come to do. Yet she looked at this length of lace, stretching away and coiling into a senseless mass in a roll of silks in a box, as though it were very strange. What had lace to do with prison? With good and bad? Couldn't lace even escape this defiling exposition? Hereafter Varra knew that lace would be something that she could no longer wear. She had thought dully that inanimate objects could not be contaminated, could have nothing in common with human beings; that was neither here nor there. She closed her eyes.

She could hear a steady droning, the shuffling of feet, a half-suppressed sob. She opened her eyes. The Pole was being led away by an officer, and on this side near her, a woman had arisen weeping. Something rose in Varra's throat—it was her grief. Something dropped down into her throat—it was her tears. She must not cry. If she had wept, she would have been a coward. At that moment, she heard the names of Karl and Monk.

She half-started to her feet! Several heads turned toward her, and someone whispered: "A relative, probably."

Yes, that was Karl; that black, curly hair was Karl's, but why did he hang his head? She did not even look toward Monk. She was angry because they must be hurting Karl where they gripped his arms on either side. Yes, she must get up now. She got up, holding the box in her hand. She heard someone saying: "Is your name Karl Handmann?" And she saw Karl move, but she could not hear his answer. Then again the same voice: "And you, Monk Price?" And she heard Monk answering, loud and with his usual bravado: "That's me."

She was down by the railing now. Her heart was pounding terribly. God! was bravery as cruel as this? She held the yellow box out in front of her as though this were her first duty. Someone laid a hand on her. She heard her own voice, "I am coming, Karl." She saw him turn around. She saw the judge's astonished eyes. The clerks paused, the stenographer, without raising his head, waited for the next remark.

Now, now she must be brave. She was going to show Karl and all the world what she was made of—the stuff—what was it—iron—oh, yes, she was made of iron. Everything went black. She began again: "I—your Honor—I." She shook her head, laughed a little and turned abruptly, holding the box. "I can't," she said, and slid to her knees.

She heard the noise subsiding, the fluttering of paper cease. The footsteps no longer moved around her. She heard only the clock striking, but she could not move. Perhaps she was dying.

She came to. Several men were plying her with water. The court attendant was back at his place. She heard the people walking again. She got to her feet.

"How do you feel now?" someone asked her, and someone else said softly: "Poor girl, was he your sweetheart or a brother?"

Varra opened her mouth. "Did—did he get off?" They seemed afraid to tell her something, and she demanded sharply in that voice she used to the children: "Come, come! Tell me."

"No. The little one with black, curly hair got—got several years."

"But," someone else chimed in, thinking it might comfort her, "the other one's case, Monk, has been suspended for a further hearing. He made a very good plea for himself—lively, rather impudent, but he made some laugh. That always helps."

Varra turned slowly to the steps and stood there staring out into the day. She was not thinking about Monk nor about Karl. She was thinking about herself. After all, she was a coward. She could kill spiders and hold hot frying pans and save birds, but she was nothing more, a small town brave—a woman without real courage, something to despise, something to hate. God, how she hated herself—how she hated those people who had begun this defeat, those people who had started it all by praising her—oh, she was horrible.

She was hungry and turned in at one of the dirty coffee stalls. She looked in the mirror—yes, she thought herself still beautiful, but now that was all.

She knew that Karl was innocent—she had seen it in his eyes. And she knew that Monk was all that was low and base and mean. She felt that he had drawn Karl into this to save his own skin. What an ugly beast he was, how red the tips of his ears had been that moment in court when she had looked at him.

She began to justify herself. Could she have confessed to something she had not done to save Karl, who wasn't guilty? No, a thousand times no. Why? Because it would have placed her below him. It would have made her something vicious and criminal. She would have allied herself to save him (it's true) with all the dirt and filth that was in that corrupt body of Monk. How could she have done this? Would he still have loved her?

Perhaps the sacrifice would have been too splendid, and besides he would have known that she wasn't really guilty. Perhaps, too, he would have denied her, refused her sacrifice. Then, what a beautiful thing it would have been. Perhaps he would have gotten off altogether and she also. How wonderful that would have been! And then he would have said to her again, "I love you because you are brave more than for anything else."

And now he had got several years, and Monk was as yet unsentenced.

When she reached home, she trembled, as though the street must already know her for what she was. She crept to her room, fearing that she would waken the family, and opened the door carefully, hardly daring to breathe. She undressed slowly, standing in the middle of the room. She got into bed as she had never gotten into it since she was a child, furtively, with a crouching movement, and drew the sheets over her throat.

She lay there, staring into the darkness—yes, that was it, that was the reason that she had failed, because she could not make herself seem so low, so mean, so petty before Karl, who was really good and clean and strong.

But what hurt most was her lost pride in herself; this was terrible. All through the night she kept saying to herself, "What must I do now?"

She got up again, lighting a candle. Was she still beautiful? People had called her ugly—she grinned at herself in the mirror. No, she was really ugly. She blew the light out, then lit it again. "How can I tell if I am ugly or handsome if I make faces?" She looked. She saw her face, a rigid, set, white thing shining out of the glass at her. No, she was not so bad.

She went back to the cot and sat on it, her bare feet touching the floor. Was there anything that she could do yet? She decided that she was not really good looking at all, and now she was not even brave.

She could not cry. She said these things to herself, half aloud; still, they did not make her wince—neither beautiful nor brave—ugly, a coward. Yet she loved Karl—she hated Monk. She was more like Monk after all—quite a lot like Monk.

She fell asleep.

The next afternoon when Monk's case came up, a woman holding a yellow box walked briskly into the court and down the aisle. The attendant went after her. This time he did not like something in her step.

She spoke in a loud, resolute, almost coarse voice, directly at the judge, paying no attention whatsoever to Monk.

And this time she went through with it.

When, with extreme reluctance, Monk was released, she did not even look at him. Instead, she smiled and asked for a mirror. People moved aside to let the slimy, ugly body of Monk pass, but Varra was paying no attention to them. She put down the pocket glass and said hurriedly, softly, "No, I am really quite ugly."

She had forgotten Karl, she had forgotten Monk. She looked at the black curtains with their heavy tassels.

Monsieur Ampee

Step upon a worm and the worm becomes a butterfly—Ampee, the unkown, suddenly and with a supreme gesture, took what had been a tradesman's nose out of his wine cup to discover that it was looked upon as a feature of not only rare excellence, but of superior distinction.

Ampee had the worm's nature. Had he done what worms are supposed to do—in other words, had he "turned"—those watching the convulsion would not have been very pleased with the hitherto unseen surface thus exposed. Ampee was not the insinuating, crawling, slimy type; he was, rather, the coldest of persons, theoretical, persistent, quiet—one of those men who live out their forty years or so as one wears their only coat, carefully, with seeming indifference, but sending it to be cleaned and pressed once in a while, and ever as it wears out having it patched and turned and mended—with the same finish in view—a coat that had once been of one piece and had come to an end of many pieces; a life that had once been just a life and had ended as a crowd—for Ampee could not have laid his hand on anything in himself that he did not eventually know for some one else's.

Ampee had lived in a sort of obscure comfort. His wife, Lyda, had long ago submerged herself. She had been an almost aristocratic lady when Ampee had married her, a woman who had always taken care to dress simply, like the queen, to act as artificially as her frank nature would permit,

146

and to live all the necessary lies that keep a household from becoming an item in the paper and the occupants from the public eye.

He looked upon his wife as upon the public. She was what all the world was—instead of buying a morning paper, he had taken Lyda to church with him and married her—thus he had subscribed to the events of the day with a wedding certificate; instead of propping up the paper of a morning, he looked at his wife. It was a saving, too. She lived as the mass lived, on air existing plain, and she complained not in a dangerous but a human way.

She had borne him three children as the world bore children. He was amused at her docility and her helplessness. She subscribed to things that the world in general subscribe to; and she renounced the usual things that are deemed injurious to the world as a rising generation. She looked to evolution and the future with an ant-like perseverance. She hurried her children into the best of health as an ant stores away food for a day to come, or as a fowl is placed on a block of ice. And she shed over them only those numbered tears that the world has discovered to be absolutely necessary for the preservation of a sufficient quantity of regret to insure tact and feeling among people who rely on the existence of those they move among.

Yet Lyda was honest, was faithful, was as happy as the people in general are happy. She, on her side, looked upon her husband as a great phenomenon, the question beyond answer, the problem without a possibility of a final footing

147

up—he represented inexorable and unending time, and in acknowledging this she acknowledged that time would never rise above what was petty, self-seeking and indifferent. Ampee lived among his fellow beings as though he were the only pardonable mistake among a million errors.

Ampee had been successful in a certain way—his business had grown and prospered quietly, he had achieved a fair income, and no place on men's tongues was set aside for his name. This he had taken good care of. A man with ambitions in a mercantile line could not afford to be personally re- nowned as the revolutionists were renowned, or as artists and bohemians in general were renowned.

He drank excellent wines and contented himself with being ugly and common; indeed he would have regretted extremely any exceptional trait or feature. He was glad that his physique was of an appropriate and unnoticeable quality. He wanted to attract as little attention to himself as a soldier wants to be conspicuous; he had as usual the obscure exterior that is required of those who go out to conquer.

Ampee had only one enemy. This was Fago, whom he called "the Nihilist," because Fago spoke occasionally of "the people" in a tone of voice that had no quality of business about it. He distrusted Fago because Fago was one of those men who could talk for half an hour about civilization without once making any allusion to their pockets, who could hold a cool argument about any subject without once bringing in profit or loss.

And then, to make it worse, Fago was owner of a rival store. Ampee had gone in for a side branch, the selling of wines, to outdo this same Fago, who had his chief trade on his excellence in his bottled produce. Still Fago had kept his customers, and Ampee had racked his mind for a solution. This was in 1842. In the Summer of 1846 Ampee bought a vineyard, set a caretaker on the place, ate a good dinner, and approached his wife.

"Lyda," he said, looking at her with the judicial eye that one turns upon a crowd, "what do you think of what I have done today?"

Lyda had long ago, probably with the birth of the second child, forgotten how the queen dressed, and no longer relied on her looks. She had only a smattering of her best quality left, her honesty—and this was subject to her fatigue and her nervousness.

"I have bought up a little vineyard," he continued. "Something like ten or twelve hundred bottles of wine should be the result. Only I have yet to install new machinery and labor, and to pay off the mortgage. To do that, I need money."

He never smoked, because it tainted his breads and cheeses. He never walked around to ease his tension, because Lyda had a habit of saying: "Sh-h, Ampee, the cakes are in the oven and you will certainly make them fall." On the other hand, he did not like a man who rubbed his hands together or bit his nails, because this was commonly called the habit of a shifty nature, and he wanted no such speculations going abroad in connection with his daily habits. Instead, Ampee would see how long he could hold his eyes very wide open without flickering the lashes; a prolonged, steady gaze was well received, and was the work of an honest, well-meaning man.

149

In this way he stared at his wife, and she, in turn, looked down, as she always did on such occasions. His eyes gave her a sad, expectant feeling of failure; she was always fearing that Ampee would at some inopportune moment fail, and these lids would fall with a suddenness and a finality that would leave no further doubt in the world's eyes of the subterfuge of their owner.

"What are your plans?"

"Start a corporation, consisting of our two selves; call it something with a sound of reliability about it, and sell shares."

"At how much per head?" She had a practical streak in her as well as others, and at times, if she was occupied in darning, she let her sense of fair play fall a little in the background, because the very fact that she had still to mend and parch reminded her that they were not quite as well off as they should be, if only for the good of their children.

"Oh, that can be settled later."

"And when would the stockholders receive their first dividend?"

"Plenty of time, plenty of time. Don't you think I will act squarely?" he added, fixing her finger with his wideset eyes. He laughed, too, without much facial exertion, pleasantly, hopefully.

Whenever Ampee set out to cheat the people, he always gave his wife some little present; he was kinder, too. He went so far as to kiss her. On the day following, she found a gold piece beneath her plate, and somehow she forgot to thank him.

During the two years that followed, Fago was slowly pressed out of the lead. He fell back; people began to turn toward Ampee's cellars. They talked of the flavor of the most excellent wine and waited hopefully for the day when their shares would show cash returns.

Ampee began to cultivate Fago's friendship: he feared him. This was an unexpected feeling for Ampee. He almost regretted having put himself in a position where he feared.

Fago had begun to doubt Ampee. He could see that there was some sort of swindle beneath the whole thing, and he felt a little contemptuous when now he saw Ampee standing in his doorway, or when he heard a customer make remarks upon the superior quality of Ampee's wine.

And then, Fago had been changing, too, as Ampee changed. As Ampee grew gross and expectant, Fago began to doubt. He grew restless and he turned over in his honest head many an old idea. Sometimes this had a most astonishing effect. In altering his former views he came to like people he had disliked and vice versa. He began to be dissatisfied with himself, although having to acknowledge that, for his former turn of mind, he had been all that could be expected. It seemed strange that he could find in himself two fairly decent men; he had always thought that there was only one kind of good and one kind of bad.

Then, too, Fago had allied himself with a semi-radical crowd, who came to drink in his back room. At first he had stood aloof, but finally, out of his friendliness, he had been drawn in, and now he did not care to contradict Ampee when Ampee called him "Nihilist," though Ampee's evident ignorance of just what constituted a nihilist made him smile.

Then one day the people, who had grown restive and angry at the non-existence of their hopes in the vineyard, began to demand of Ampee. He saw that it was about time to draw out with his little haul and to change his quarters or play bankrupt. Lyda had been very silent for the past few weeks, and was uncommunicative; as a thermometer she was beginning to fail him and Ampee resented her.

Sitting on the edge of his bed that night, he told her something.

"Lyda, we have come off very nicely—very nicely, indeed. What do you say if we retire into the country for a while, or take a trip abroad?"

"You are going to close the shop! You are going to swindle the people! You have never done this before, excepting in short measure. I do not like it. It does not stand in with my principle. It is a mean man's trick. It will leave you worse off in the end than you are. Let us put it entirely on a practical footing. What are you going to do when next you want to show your face?"

"Show it," he answered, looking at her fixedly.

"And what will happen to you?"

"Nothing," he answered, crossing his long legs. "Nothing ever does. This is the way all big men have started—that is, all my kind of big men."

"What do you call your kind?"

"The obscure. I am satisfied with gain in a financial way. I have no personal pride. I do not long to become one of the peerage or to hold a place in politics. Therefore, it was quite correct."

"You must take me into account. I have certain qualities. You must not overlook them."

"Such as?" There was a hint of a sneer in Ampee's face.

"I come of a good family."

"Yes, you do."

"I have my reputation for honesty."

"That too, yes."

"Well, what are you going to do with them?"

"My dear woman, you speak as though they were a stock—as though they were packages."

"Well, yes, that's so."

"I will let you keep them."

"Good of you," she answered with a touch of her old refinement. Then she broke out into stormy abuse.

"You are a pitiable thing, Monsieur Ampee, and we are not going to stand for you, I tell you. I shall tell your children what you are."

"They have guessed."

She said with a flash of sudden illumination, "Are you there?" And he sprung up, startled and puzzled and shocked. He half turned and looked at himself from the shoulder down.

"What is it?" he cried excitedly. "What is it—"

She burst into tears.

So he looked at her as she lay face to the wall. That must have been a whim of hers, calling that out, treating him as something so small that he might get lost. He stretched himself beside her and looked up at the ceiling.

He had always been able to treat his wife as one treats algebra or a simple sum; go so far, do thus and thus and it would have this and that effect. Whenever he wanted to see how far his calculations had gone, all he had to do was to add up, and this simply by the means of his wife's face, actions or phraseology. Presently, without emotion, only curious of the sum he had now to contend with, he reached his hand over and dropped his fingers into the hollows of his wife's closed eyes. He lifted them up and looked at them, spreading the fingers and closing them. They were wet with her tears. That meant that the experiment had gone up to its unanswerable quantity, i.e., that Lyda would reach reaction and come down the balance side and with a probable mistake in calculation.

But this time it did not have quite the result that he expected. She did not turn around. She continued to weep silently but firmly, as a person weeps who has a fair foundation based on a condition of long standing.

This annoyed Ampee, and to his annoyance he probably owed his life. He got up, put his dressing gown on and went downstairs to extinguish the kitchen lamp and the light in the front of the store, as was his usual custom, but which he had neglected to see to on this particular night.

Then came the explosion—a slight sound of tearing wood, a curtain caught fire from a gust from the window—and bewildered, frightened and almost paralyzed, Ampee picked himself up with the flaming curtain in his hand. He looked at it, then dashed it into a vat of wine and turned toward the stairs. He ran up them lightly, quickly, and, still running, entered his wife's room.

The floor sagged where a great hole had been torn in it near the window. The bedstead on which Lyda was lying was intact, but Lyda herself remained motionless.

He approached her half choking on a terrible thought. He

said, "Ayah," and put his hand upon her face.

So the experiment could go farther, the figures could be made to add up to an answer he had not expected.

He turned his wife's face toward him. Death from shock, probably. He hadn't expected this. He didn't like it. How in God's name had all this happened? Then it flashed through his mind. The revolutionists. Fago!

His eyelids dropped. He began to cry.

He wept as a man weeps who is terribly frightened.

Two months later, a well-known figure, a bereaved man, a broken tradesman as far as outside appearances went, but with plenty of money for drinks and such entertainment, Ampee again comes upon the scene.

He has gotten nicely out of his obligations along with the wreck of his home—the safe, everything, money, bonds, deeds, capital, all went with the rest of the things.

It does not matter who believed or who did not believe— he cast out dark hints that it was due to the "Nihilists" and those scurvy fellows the revolutionists, bohemians and writers. It does not matter to him that it was proved to be carelessness on his own or on someone else's part, due to the explosion among some cans of powder and other things kept in the cellar. No, undoubtedly it was chiefly due to the fact that as a business his had outstripped a certain man on the opposite side of the street. At this Fago did not so much as laugh, it seemed to utterly ridiculous. "You know," he said, "we don't do such dirty little tricks as cleaning rats out or stepping on worms." And strangely enough, Ampee laughed and took no offense.

Of an evening, people would nudge one another as he sat in the cafes. He had become what he had never expected to be—personally renowned through police investigation and local comment and newspaper mention. When the case finally blew over—he was willing enough—he had become quite a "Dandy" and was considered quite charming.

But one night he sat himself down among the very circle he had abused.

They held him in contempt, but liked to play with him, turning him this way and that.

They would say, "Well, how is life now, Tradesman Ampee?"

And he would slap his knee and pound his free foot, and he would light a cigarette and, waving his arms, say excellent things humorously, finally ending up on the middle of the table in a drunken dance. And one night, as he swung his arms as if they had been wings, he leaned down and whispered to Fago:

"There are some things that will not bear stirring up, my little revolutionists, and one of them is clear water." Here he shouted with laughter and then, drawing his brows together, he solemnly got down from the table amid the taunts of the group, who had overheard him.

"No," they said, "not when the water is a puddle and it stirs up mud; not when it is likely to drain off all the innocent looking surface and leaves behind the dirt." He knew that by drawing off the pure water they referred to Lyda.

He shouted: "I tell you, you will see there are some things that you can't blow up. There are some things you can't thrust your fingers into without making them worse. Listen, I'm telling you something—listen to me while I am in emotion. Go ahead, be mad, try to right things, but you see, you see—I fly. You say draw off the water, and I say beware of what is beneath the water. It is not always so pleasant to look upon. It is not always so nice—and people like to see nice things, don't they? Well, step on the worm—so." He ground his heels into an imaginary insect.

He turned away amid the shouts from the company grouped around Fago, and as they derided him on his wings, one of them asked him where he was going, and he turned his head over his shoulder and answered with fixed eyelids, "To wash my hands."

"In early youth Pilaat had been very melancholy"

The Terrorists

In early youth Pilaat had been very melancholy, though vigorous. This was due to his healthy body and to his imaginative mind.

Those people who are in the habit of assuming that a melancholy stomach must accompany a sad mind, were rather disconcerted with Pilaat's indomitable digestion, about his excesses that never gave him punishment in their passing, and about his unalterable decision to become a necessity in the community.

Then his hair had been long and his dress decidedly on the "artistic" plan. His straight nose had below it a very full and perhaps weak mouth, and above it, eyes of a strange, large and mournful turn.

Time shortened the hair a little and the mouth was covered by a graying mustache. The eyes watered easily, and sometimes, during an evening, blood veins would stretch across them.

Pilaat was no longer vigorous, though for a man of fifty odd, he was robust enough. On the other hand, his melancholy had, so people seemed to think, disappeared altogether. Those who knew him longest made the mistake of calling him "more like a human being"; and those who knew him the shortest, made the correct judgment, that he was "drinking too much."

His early love of the people had sent him toward them

eagerly. Being close to them and in with them, he learned how pitifully weak they all were, and his strong digestion made him despise them for those qualities which, somehow, he blamed on environment and not heredity, excepting as one can inherit the filth of the gutter and the starvation of the ash pile. And along with his interest, his study and his acknowledgment of its inevitablity, came this robust hate.

From speaking of the people as the "Unfortunate," he spoke of them as the "Miserable." And in the way he said this word there was no sound of pity for their sad, shabby hearts; there was only a knowledge that their garments were also shabby and mournful. Had Pilaat come from a less cleanly family, he would have loved them very strongly and gently to the end. But he had been comforted and maimed in his conceptions and his fellow love by too many clean shirts in youth. He still longed to correct things, but he wanted to correct them as one cleans up a floor, not as one binds up a wound.

He shouted because his heart was heavy. He began to awe those of his own group. Soon enough, they called him the "Terrorist," and, in the end, when he made a gesture of pity, people raised their arms to protect themselves.

He had a very young wife, a weak-chinned, small thing about 27 years old. She had been nicknamed Joan d'Arc, because of a certain pale loveliness about the frail oblong of her face. She had lost two or three teeth, and she smoked innumerable cigarettes, drank beer on half-holidays, and flirted with anyone whom she despised.

She believed in the vanity of all things and the pessimism in all things, and she wanted to annihilate any slovenly ease of mind in herself, so she deliberately set about annihilating her own soul and her own delicate, sensitive, and keen insight.

She wore heavy boots that seemed to be drawing her down; thus her five feet looked like three.

Her hair was cut short after the manner of intellectuals among the women of her set, and she wore loose and dirty blouses, smeared with paint and oil.

She was in the cafes all the afternoon from three till six, when she "cleared out" for "the pigs," the smug and respectable who brought their wives and children to dine. Again at nine she was back talking about the revolutionists.

Pilaat had written some poems and had them published obscurely; these she always carried around with her, reading them aloud or studying them nonchalantly. She had long grown tired of them, but she wanted to puzzle the strangers who filtered in, and she wanted to add, when asked about them, "By Pilaat Korb—you know, the Terrorist," never referring to the fact that he was her husband; this she left for others to whisper. She liked to be the center of whispers, for then she could be impersonal and forget herself without any danger of falling into obscurity.

Among her friends she would permit herself the pleasure of pretending to feel human suffering very deeply. She would swing her arms about, imitating Pilaat. She would lean far back in her chair as he did when he had finished a sentence as "I know, you call me crazy—but that is not all. I have a retort to make, an accusation. You, the people—what do you know?—are you not being swindled on every side, and yet you submit? Ah, fools! Fools!" he would shout. "You are always horribly conscious of your bones, and you begin to think that it is as it should be. You say this is life—bah!" He would then end up leaning far back as his wife did when she copied him, thinking that she was expressing herself. And sometimes her friends said, "Certainly, there you are," while they drank beer or devoured large, ill-shaped sandwiches.

She would say, "You wander, my poor friends, about the world like shadows. We must find you your bodies once again." She said "we" with that intonation used by agitators.

These two lived in a dismal little garret high above the rest of the sad houses of the shabby side street. The building had once been some kind of church or house of devotion, but had long ago been turned into rooms, and was now frequented by a vocalist, a violin and a piano teacher, and a few out-at-knee artists.

There was never any lock on the outer door, approached by three rickety steps. Two or three iron mailboxes clung to the walls, and in the Winter, when the wind howled hardest and the snow made park benches impossible, tramps and derelicts of all kinds would creep in here and sleep along the walls near the dry wood of the steps.

Their garret had been at one time very dignified and almost elegant, as its tall lines and its heavy wood proclaimed. Its windows and the architecture of the roof spoke of a past that had been no mean thing. Now it was like a woman who had fallen from wealth and distinction and esteem, who had lost all her admirers, but not quite all her looks, who passes her remaining days in that odd mixture of clothes that look so strange together—a silk and beribboned petticoat hidden by a calico dressing gown, a torn stocking thrust into small and delightfully fashioned slippers, a well-appointed mouth closing on crumbs. Such was the room to which of an evening Pilaat and his little wife climbed.

Sometimes the sleeping men in the hall would be awakened by their late arrival and would turn over muttering abuse, or some of them accepted Pilaat's invitation to have a drink with him.

Thus he would collect a party that often made merry until the small hours of the morning. Or Pilaat would bring some of his friends with him—they led the life of actors—sleeping into the late afternoon and staying up half or all of the night.

Toward the end of his career, Pilaat began to tear his mustache out. When remonstrated with, he would say, "I am preparing to show my teeth." He had become very nervous and excitable and unhappy. He felt that the world was not going in the direction that he had wished. It neither turned toward his solution early enough, nor did it, on the other hand, succumb to its final end, as he had predicted, soon enough for him. He was tired of living out his life and watching others live out theirs on the prescribed gradual plan. He was annoyed with the passage of time; it infuriated him that twenty-four hours were still a day and that there were seven days a week, as there had been when he was born.

He no longer wrote poetry or plays, nor did he keep up his connection with a paper which he had started, and which spoke harshly of all things. He had taken more and more to his bottle, and because he was very nervous he drank too much, and because he drank too much, he became more and more excitable.

Instead of writing his poetry, now he laid it in among the strands of his wife's hair in his occasional tender strokings, when he would call her Little One and, sometimes, Sniffle Snuffle, when he would burst out laughing heartily at her disconcerted countenance. She knew well enough that Pilaat saw through her would-be ferocity and her assumed interest in the world. Afer all, she was only a little girl who, because she was interested, thought that she must assume fury, and because she was too lazy to dress her hair after the fashion, cut it off.

Yet there was something strange about Pilaat's wife. She did not like the society of silly and vain women, and she did turn most naturally to such men as her husband moved among. Perhaps it started in a torn shoe and a consciousness that only in such society are shoes valued more for the pass they have come to than from what they had been originally.

She had never much sympathy for "society," and a marriage of money disgusted her, though her family had, in the beginning, some such vain ideas about her. They were respectable people who owned a little estate somewhere near the sea, and who had been dropped in successive generations into the midst of old and tarnished jewelry comprising the family splendor. Most of this they had given to their daughter when they had their first ambitions in the way of a well-to-do doctor in the village, and which their daughter had promptly pawned. Sometimes, it is true, this jewelry would come back, piece by piece, and appear on her wrist or about her neck or from her ears, and at such times she drew a little aside from her husband and his friends, and would sit dreaming in a corner, her red wrists about her little crooked knees.

On one such a night as this Pilaat had acted very strangely indeed. He had passed several morose hours by himself, and finally, at a cafe located his wife, wearing this mysterious and migratory jewelry.

The sight of these gems and silvers always put him into a passion either of avarice or contempt—he would get hold of them and realize money on the spot, or he would very bitterly place them on the table before him and solemnly demand that they be cleared away with the rest of the "rubbish."

His wife would become silent, smiling a little, her head thrown back. Or, if the waiter did make a motion to sweep the trinkets away, she would say in a loud voice, "Yes, that's right: take them away. Feed them to the chickens or make a meal off them. I'm tired of supporting them." Then Pilaat cried in a terrible fury, catching the dazed waiter by the wrist and swearing at the top of his voice in Rumanian, Italian and French, saying that he was being treated like a man "who has not come honestly by his decorations."

From this, he went off into a melancholy reverie. He answered nothing in the way of a question, and ordered innumerable bottles of wine.

When, accompanied by three of four friends, they finally reached their house, Pilaat threatened to kill the vocalist who was teaching someone to sing in the room below them, it being half-past twelve.

"What is all that racket about?" he demanded, flying down

the steps and pounding on the door of the vocalist's room. A thin, yellow-faced woman, the vocalist in question, opened the door sharply, thrust her head out, and said: "Be off with you, you lazy vagabond. In my country such people as you would be locked up."

Pilaat struck his chest with his fist. "Locked up, is it?" he demanded, smiling fiercely. "Locked up, is it? That is what I have against this country. They do not let you go home unless you commit something that makes you a little ashamed to say 'How do you do?' to the mother of all things, the cell."

She slammed the door on the implication. "You're crazy!" Pilaat flew back upstairs, shouting: "Crazy! and did I not warn you that I was crazy, you poor, senseless thing? Did I not give myself full credit for it in the very beginning? But does that make it necessary for me to be tortured with the horrible sounds issuing from such lovely throats as Maria's (the pupil who took the vocal lessons)? And must I forever regret the inferiority of the things Maria is forced to swallow, and of the noise Maria tosses from out her little throat?"

He was in the middle of the room by this time, and much amused his friends. His wife leaned back in the corner and twisted the bracelets around and around, blinking her eyelids and shuffling with her feet.

"What is it you would do with the little Maria if you had her and could dispose of her case as you would, eh?" inquired one man, with a bristling beard and an odor about him of tar.

"What would I do?" demanded Pilaat, seating himself with his back to the fire. "I would have her singing in Paradise by dawn. After all, I am a man of force. Some day I shall march upon the town and shall show you. It's about time for an uprising when little girls think they can sing and young men think they can govern."

"Ah, well, it's a dull season; the Autumn is nearly here."

"Autumn," retorted Pilaat, flourishing his arm, "is the season for destruction—but we are weak, miserable creatures, and we leave to nature all the tearing down of the scenery, and to her we leave all the building up of the same scenery next year and the year after for interminable and tireless and wearisome years."

"Well?"

"I would tear down the scenery better than all of them," he said irrelevantly. "Than all of them I would rip the whole existing plan of nature to pieces. How she would shiver, how she would implore. But I should have no mercy. No, not even when she got upon her knees and wept at my feet and covered them with her insufferable tears. I would invite her to suicide. I would mock at the stains upon her cheeks. I would glory at the dirt on the imploring knees. I would laugh aloud, and shake her by those horrible, ample shoulders of hers, and would cry out to her, 'Now die, die; we do not care! Tear the little leaves out of your heart. We are in need of them for a bed. Weep; we need a drink. Destroy yourself, for we need a harp on which to sing the song of freedom.' " He had become half drunk with his frenzy, and he stood up.

"I tell you, I would say to her: 'We are tired of you. I, Pilaat, am tired of you, and she, my little girl, is tired of you, and Maria is tired of you. We are tired of your spontaneity and your persistency and your punctuality. We want to see you dead and smouldering. What will we do? We will thrust our feet into your heart because they are cold, and our hands we

will warm at your palms. And we will shake them at your death, saying: "At last you have accomplished more than seasons and beauty; you have created destruction." We can no longer rise in the morning and say, "Behold, the sun has arisen." We shall no longer send our children to school to learn mathematics. We shall never be connected with you any longer as the outcome of your whims. We are set free—thus." ' "
He snapped his fingers and executed a pirouette on his heel, and sat down, discussing the feasibility of destruction on a large scale.

His wife still blinked her eyes in the corner, and continued to roll her bracelets. The whole room had such a menacing aspect, such a sad and gloomy atmosphere, and contained so many odors and voices that she was annoyed and wanted to sleep. Sleep had overcome one of the men who leaned against a table; his head had fallen forward and he snored a little.

In the other corner of the room, the conversation had taken a decidedly revolutionary turn. They were beginning to talk of besieging the town. Names were mentioned as persons to destroy. They began to collect things that would do as missiles.

The room began to bristle. Dark beards stood out as though their wearers had been scratched. Lips protruded, ears trembled, the very beards began to shake. Fists doubled up, eyes sparkled, and the tongue knew no forbidden thing. There was something at once terrible and beautiful about these men, who, rising, suddenly turned for a moment toward the old boards of that room such a searching and melancholy gaze that tatters and misery might have seemed for one instant something splendid.

"Eh, it will be magnificent. In the dawn we shall do it. In the dawn we shall creep forth to make the world better for men. They will see us coming, creeping on all fours, and they will say, 'Here are the rats.' They shall learn what rats can do." Some of the men stretched a little among the empty bottles. Pilaat began to drowse, a heavy paperweight in his hand. John, his bosom friend, leaned near with the broken leg of a chair firmly clutched in his hand, and he whispered a little to make it more menacing.

The fire had died down and barely a light flickered. Pilaat's head fell forward on his chest. The bristling beards one by one relaxed and rested once more down in smooth, silky lines. Deep breathing took the place of cries, oaths, imprecations. Pilaat's wife stirred uneasily in her corner, dreaming, her hand over her bracelets.

She woke up—it was midday. She looked out into the street. A postman was standing on the steps of the door opposite, and a woman with a baby in pink ribbons moved slowly out toward the park.

She stumbled over Pilaat and two or three of the men huddled together for warmth. All of them, in their sleep, had moved away from those things that they had collected as weapons. They had rolled onto them, and they found that they hurt and were uncomfortable. The chair leg lay beside the paperweight. She stretched, opened her mouth, and yawned. She looked about for a cigarette stub, and found it, lighting it slowly. She prepared the little oil stove for the reception of the old and stained coffeepot. She looked out of the window again; it was a splendid day. She thought of her favorite cafe, and she smiled as she contemplated one or two new phrases she would use in relation to life. She put Pilaat's book in her pocket. The coffee began to boil.

A Night in the Woods

For Trenchard the town jail represented freedom he had always wanted so passionately, communal freedom that those enjoying it call social boredom. To him who must ever serve in his little cellar where he baked bread, this square and rickety edifice seemed something holy, until the day he and his wife got locked up in it only to discover that they were the only transgressors in a community of five thousand inhabitants—and this rather spoiled matters.

Jennie and he had been married something like those proverbial happy thirty years or so. They were both stout, small, and good natured. They were both gentle with downy complexions and easy smiles. They were both so exactly suited to each other that it seemed as though they must have been born somewhere in a nest together.

Both of them came originally from the south of France; neither of them remembered much about it, though they would cry excitedly, "Ah, what a world that was, my dear. Full of sunlight and leaves, upturned earth and flowers."

Both of them throughout their married existence had spoken almost reverently about freedom—meaning such freedom as these youthful memories cast back—the freedom of the out-of-doors.

Jennie could have adapted herself to things as they were if it had not been for her loyalty to Trenchard. True, she often looked out into the streets to breathe in the beauties of the newly budded trees that flanked the library on either side, but it was a passive sort of longing that would have gone with her to the grave but for the corresponding longing in her husband's breast.

They had no children to free them with the delightful bondage of new youth; they had no relatives and no very close friends saving their dog Pontz. They lived in a world of exactly one—for Jennie Trenchard, for Trenchard Jennie, with their love for their dog entering in as part of them.

In youth Jennie had been round, rosy, kind, of quick action and of slow mind. She had been born to a world of chickens and ducks, of cows and horses and casual Springs and casual Autumns. She had been pig-tailed then, had worn blue pinafores and had been the quietest girl in school. When the boys teased her she would frown a little; when they would pull her braids she would turn her head slowly and say nothing very marked in contempt, but very hesitant in coming. She would never cry, never whine, never complain. Finally, they let her alone, this sort of young person being the bane of a naughty boy's existence.

In youth Trenchard had been small also, plump, exceedingly good natured, but quick tempered. He was slow with his lessons, dreamy in his method and much petted by his parents.

He had large and thick lidded eyes and the whitest of skins. His mouth and nose were like something against a hard and determined wall. The nose pugged abruptly.

She was still blonde, though turning to something paler. He still possessed black hair, though of late years it had begun to curl a little, the only sign that he had grown up, he would say, and she: "You are going to be still younger than when you were born, my dear."

Of course, their tempers were not always mild. They had some few fallings out as is not only necessary, but customary in good families. He could not smoke, therefore he chewed. She had forgiven him long ago for this "filthy trick, never indulged in by my father." She could not sew, but he had forgiven her, though "all the women in my family had been par excellence at needlework."

At times Trenchard would fall into a morose silence; then Jennie smiled and served the customers herself. At night, when the oven door shone out like the bleeding mouth of some demon, Trenchard, stripped to the waist, pulled out little biscuits for the morning trade. His wife would say, quite resolutely: "My dear, you are working too hard. There is plenty of time and money now for both our old age and a little vacation."

He would shake his head.

"Yes, you need a little rest," and he would always add:

"Bah, I need freedom."

She would sit down resting her hands on the check of her apron, saying, "Well then, your freedom; let us buy a little land."

"Where from? We have not enough capital."

"Let us venture," she would say.

"One may speculate before the age of twenty, but not after," he would answer. And so the days would pass with the little longings of both stilled by the respective kindnesses and forethought of each for them.

And then the crash comes. A man and his wife somewhere on the border of town die suddenly, and the cause has been traced back to poison found in a loaf of bread. As Jennie and Trenchard are the only bakers in the town, they are immediately pounced upon by the marshal, and both of them landed securely in that very jail that Trenchard had been longing to inhabit.

Like little birds they begin to pick at each other, questioning, talking, laughing, weeping. Trenchard always weeps easily; now his face is composed of laughter, tears, astonishment and fear, pleasure and disappointment.

"Is this the place," he seems to say as he turns around and around in what is like an ordinary room with a few rusty bars up at the windows.

Impossible, he begins to laugh. "My dear Jennie," he says with great excitement, "here is the freedom and the holiday we have been talking about."

"Do not laugh," she answers severely, "there is real danger here. We have been accused of a frightful thing—do you understand?" Here she catches him by the sleeve and pulls at it. "We are in for murder—poisoning. Of course," she adds logically, "we did not do it, so that's off our minds. But perhaps they will think we did all the same, and then we die—yes, assuredly we die, little Trenchard, and I do not like to think of that so soon."

"Eh, that's so." He sits down and begins to cry again heartily in great sobs. Jennie, dry-eyed and calm, folds her hands over her apron as she has so often done in the little shop.

"What shall we do?"

"There is nothing to do."

As if this had struck a terrible pang to his ear, Trenchard begins to weep afresh, while Jennie pats him on the shoulder. "There, there," she says comfortingly, "you must remember, little one, that all things come to all men, or so they say. And here we are."

"But, Jennie, we may be hung."

"Very true."

"But it is terrible. We must do something. Are there no ways in the world of showing these people that we did not poison the bread?"

"Oh yes, there are a lot of ways, if they will let us show them."

"Then let us do it immediately." He stands up at this and starts for the door.

"The door is locked, Trenchard. At last you know what it is like to be in jail."

"You need not remind me."

"I do not want you to forget."

"Is it you, Jennie, who have held me back always?"

"What do you mean?"

"It is because of you that I have never had my freedom, my little beloved freedom, the love of my heart."

"Trenchard, you are a wretch."

"Jennie, you are a willful and bad woman."

Whereat they both fall to weeping and kissing each other and patting each other as if they were trying to mend a broken image, something they have reared up in their thirty years of arried life.

The night has begun to fall in great shadows, as though it, too, were in prison. The air has begun to chill, for it is late Summer, and the two cling closer together, waiting for the tread of the watchman.

Trenchard begins to dream—not far away are the woods, the great, clean, sheltering woods, with the moss and the leaves that he has so often longed to explore, but which he has never had time to so much as visit. Jennie begins to worry about the biscuits that had been left to rise.

From the window, he can see the great pines, and beyond this, the dying sun. A little puff of fresh air blows against his cheek and he sighs, feeling for his tobacco. He bites off a little piece and begins to chew slowly.

"Life is not freedom after all, eh, Jennie?" She shakes her head, still worrying about the biscuits.

Leaning close to the bars of the window, he looks away into the great dark and the greater silence of the woods. A few wild birds, startled by nightfall, circle far overhead, calling out in a lonely and barren way, as they descend into the shelter of the forest.

Suddenly Trenchard says: "Jennie," stealthily, "we are going to escape."

There is more in this one word "escape" than just the meaning that he would seem to give it! There is in it all the longing of their lives, for that remembered freedom of their youth, the play-time when they were both too young to appreciate, but also too young to forget.

"Is there a way?"

He says grandly: "I shall make a way."

And he does. Standing on tip-toes, he goes about the worm-eaten and rickety room, feeling along the floor, looking up at the ceiling, testing it with his eyes.

"Try the window."

He is in an ecstasy of anticipation of a romance that at last he shall know the taste and the smell of as he tries the window bars, which shake in their sockets, but do not bend.

Alas, it is fruitless; but not so the door. Jennie, going boldly up to it, as small children go up to what sometimes they fear, to bully it, shakes it, only to have the door open slowly with a creaking noise that had only a few moments before been the sound of bondage.

They peer out into the darkness. Someone snores gently. They begin to run, clumsily at first and then swifter. Toward the shadows of the woods, toward the great out-of-doors and that great freedom. Jennie had not forgotten the biscuits, however, and pants out: "Hadn't we better go back to the shop, Trenchard, and see to the dough?" But he does not hear her; his soul is filled with the new freedom, his first breath of night air and the trees in thirty years.

He shivers a little. "Isn't it glorious?" And she says, "Yes, it is lovely." And they run on.

But they cannot run very far, because, after all, they are very old for such things, and it is for Trenchard, chew or flight; and you must remember that tobacco is a thirty years' habit, and longing for freedom only a thirty years' desire, and the one is always stronger than the other.

They fall beside a clump of bushes.

The smell of fresh sod and moss comes to their nostrils, the odor of a crushed flower, of a few bleeding berries. The sound in the air of leaves and wind seems good. The birds that Trenchard had watched have now disappeared altogether, and everything is still save something moving under earth and the restless noises of a forest that grows always, leaving the earth for the air.

Presently they move on again, striking deeper into the forest where pursuit is almost impossible. They go down on hands and knees and creep; they fall on their faces once or twice, and Jennie whispers, "That time I kissed the earth."

It is chilly, even colder than they expected, and they have no shelter save the bushes under which they lie and the coat of Trenchard.

"Do you think," she begins, "that they will ever find us here?"

He says grandly: "I doubt it."

"But what about our shop?"

"How could we return to that—we are fugitives, don't you understand, Jennie?"

"Yes," she says, "I understand." But she doesn't, and she looks at Trenchard with sorrowful eyes, thinking how much, indeed, he must have longed for his freedom.

"But what would they do to us?"

"Do you know the import of the offense charged against us?"

"Yes, I know."

"Then you know what they will do with us."

"We will die."

"Yes, we will die—provided they catch us."

"Will they catch us, Trenchard?"

"I do not know—why do you worry? We are at present free, Jennie. Lie down and look at the stars."

"I can't lie down!" she cries, suddenly, catching hold of Trenchard. "What if you should get caught and killed, and I also?"

"No, no, it is all right; we shan't be."

"But perhaps?"

Presently they both start up.

"What was that?"

"It sounded like a dog barking."

"And that?"

"We are being pursued already," he says drearily, getting once more to his knees. "Let us move on."

They hear the dog barking again, nearer now and plainly gaining on them.

"Hark!" Jennie exlaims. "It sounds like our Pontz."

"I left him in the cellar. He will betray us—our child will surely betray us."

They hear him so near now that they think he must be beside them, but it was not so. In a moment more, however, Pontz flings his heavy white body upon them, yelping in little short, mad cries of delight—leaping up about them, licking their hands and faces.

Then they hear men's voices.

"Ah, mon Dieu!" they both exclaim. "The little one has betrayed us already."

Trenchard, on his knees, tries to hold the mouth of Pontz close. "Not yet," he whispers.

Pontz begins to whine, to twist—escaping again he barks louder, more joyfully.

"It must be," Trenchard says, and catches the dog by the throat. He sets his hands about him, presses slowly, and as he presses tears come into his eyes. Jennie sits forward, her hands in her lap. She begins to count the squares in her apron. Presently they begin to dig.

Will they have time to bury him—their little one—so glad to see them, so happy, so faithful?

No. They are too exhausted. Finally they lie down beside the body of the dead Pontz.

"Will they find us?"

"Probably."

"Isn't that a lantern light?"

"Yes, I think it is."

"It has cost us dear, Trenchard."

"But it is freedom—for a little while."

"Wouldn't it be better to die now—than later—when—"

"No. Just lie here. This is beautiful."

"It is terrible."

He sits up suddenly and savagely.

"Let them think we are happy, contented."

"I can hear what they are saying, Trenchard; they are almost upon us."

"Now let us lie still—this is freedom."

This book was set in Souvenir type at The Writer's Center,
Glen Echo, Maryland.

Printed by McNaughton & Gunn, Ann Arbor, Michigan.